GUT IT OUT . . .

Cord cocked his rifle again just as he heard his bullet smack into flesh.

Aikens let out a grunt and his hand slipped from the lever as pain shot through his body in a rush of muscle contractions and screaming nerve endings.

He doubled over as the bullet ripped through his abdomen and smashed a cup-sized hole out his back. His brain flashed with pain signals and he expelled air from his mouth in a guttural grunt. The ground threatened to rush up to him and topple him backward.

He slumped down, braced by his legs, and his rifle fell from his hand. He clawed for his pistol as Cord approached.

"You might think a second or two before you draw that pistol," Cord said.

"Damn your hide," Aikens growled.

His fingers wrapped around the butt of his pistol, but he struggled to tighten them or draw his weapon. Blood spurted from his abdomen and he showed signs of weakening.

Cord kept his rifle aimed at Aikens as he strode ever closer toward him.

"You gutshot me, Wild."

THE
WILD
GUN

JORY SHERMAN

B

BERKLEY BOOKS, NEW YORK

THE BERKLEY PUBLISHING GROUP
Published by the Penguin Group
Penguin Group (USA) LLC
375 Hudson Street, New York, New York 10014

USA • Canada • UK • Ireland • Australia • New Zealand • India • South Africa • China

penguin.com

A Penguin Random House Company

THE WILD GUN

A Berkley Book / published by arrangement with the author

For information, address: The Berkley Publishing Group,
a division of Penguin Group (USA) LLC,
375 Hudson Street, New York, New York 10014.

ISBN: 978-0-425-27240-4

PUBLISHING HISTORY
Berkley mass-market edition / July 2014

PRINTED IN THE UNITED STATES OF AMERICA

10   9   8   7   6   5   4   3   2   1

Cover illustration by Bill Angresano.
Cover design by Diana Kolsky.
Interior text design by Kelly Lipovich.

ONE

Two riders on shod horses. Four unshod horses. Four *stolen* horses. One stallion and three mares. One of the mares was in season. One was carrying a foal.

The tracks were plain to see in the Medicine Bows. All were headed toward the Snowy Range at a slow pace. That was because the stud was mounting the mare in heat every so often.

Cordwainer Wild chewed on the tail end of a rhubarb stalk as he studied the tracks, estimated their age. Less than an hour fresh, now that he had almost caught up with the two rustlers.

A six-hour drive from Jesse Barnes's JB Ranch in Wyoming Territory. A hard ride for Cord, but one he was used to and took in stride.

There was an added urgency to his mission to catch up to the two rustlers.

A boy, barely fifteen, lay dead in the barn on the JB spread. Billy Wheeler, as innocent and defenseless as a fledgling mountain partridge chick.

Cord leaned to one side. His six foot four stature made it easier for him to study the tracks as he rode. So far, the rustlers had shown no signs of evasion. They followed a well-worn game trail that echoed the tracks they had made when they had come two years before to Wesley Gannon's 2Bar2 Ranch in the foothills of the Medicine Bows.

The two horse thieves had made the same ride before, not just to Gannon's ranch, but to others that lay between Cheyenne and Laramie. Those two, or two others cut from the same sorry bolt of cloth.

The tracks veered off the game trail. One or more of the horses had spooked.

Cord sat up straight in the saddle and sniffed the thin mountain air.

Bear scat.

He glanced in the direction of the scent and saw an outcropping of limestone upslope from where he rode.

The bear smell had spooked the horses, and he had to pat Windmill's neck to keep him from bolting away from the strong scent. The dark sorrel snorted as if to spray the cloying aroma from his rubbery nostrils, and he bowed his neck in protest. But the horse held steady as they rode on until Cord saw the horse droppings where at least two of the horses had heeded a call to nature.

He smelled that pungent aroma, too, and saw tiny wisps of mist from the droppings that told him he was getting close.

He slowed Windmill as he gazed ahead. He knew that the closer he got to the two horse thieves, the more dangerous it would be for him. Beyond the outcroppings, the pines and firs were thick and he saw deadfalls scattered amid the under-brush. The trail angled downward a few yards ahead, down toward water where the deer, elk, rabbits, wolves, coyotes, and other critters drank before bedding down for the day. The game trail was littered with animal tracks. These were mixed in and struck over by iron hooves and the unshod horses, but still visible.

A highway through the timber.

The men he tracked were well-known in Cheyenne. They were men he had seen before in the saloons and in jail.

They worked for a man named Horace Weatherall, a horse breeder and cattle rancher who had done prison time for embezzlement, but kept some of the money he had stolen and bought a ranch under suspicious circumstances some three or four years ago, the 2Bar2, from a struggling cattle-man named Gannon. Gannon had lost almost his entire herd of Herefords in a blizzard two years earlier.

There were those who swore that Wes's herd had been chased into the Snowy Range by night riders whose faces were never seen. There were suspicions, but the law could not prove anything. So Horace had bought the ranch for a song. Some said he only paid Wes a small amount of money, promising him the balance within a year's time.

Wes never lived long enough to get the money owed him. He was found out on the prairie, beaten to death.

But Horace had a bona fide bill of sale and so he took over the 2Bar2.

Cord had his own suspicions. There was a man who swore he had seen Wes thrown from his horse and stomped on by a herd of antelope.

The story sounded far-fetched to Cord, too, but again, there was no proof to counter the claim.

Except that the man who claimed to be an eyewitness worked for Horace and was surely one of the men Cord now tracked.

He thought the man's name was Larry Dolan. And the other man likely riding with him was a well-known gunfighter from St. Louis named Lester Aikens, who had more aliases than the entire town of Guthrie, Oklahoma.

The names of the thieves and their boss ran through Cord's mind like ripples in a stream. And he also thought of the dead boy, the senselessness of it. His anger thrashed at those ripples of thought, and he crunched down on the rhubarb and balled up a fist.

A large blue spruce blocked his view, but the game path wound around it and angled downslope toward the creek. He approached the spruce with an added wariness. A man, or two, could be just beyond it, waiting in ambush.

He looked at Windmill's ears for any warning signs. The horse was attuned to every movement, every sound. Windmill could smell danger, too. But the horse was calm, and Cord gave him his head to continue down the game trail.

Just beyond the blue spruce with its lush, thick boughs, he saw where one man had left the trail. The other had gone on down toward the creek, the four horses in tow.

Cord stiffened in the saddle.

The horse thieves likely knew he was on their trail. He glanced down and saw the circles of dark stains where the horses had urinated. A thin scrim of steam rose from the dimples in the dirt.

The outlaws had been there scant moments before. And one of them was circling to pick up his back trail.

He knew which one, too.

Lester Aikens. He was the more skilled killer of the two. The most treacherous.

Cord stayed behind the spruce, then edged forward to look upslope to see if there was any movement, any sign of where Aikens might be.

Windmill whickered softly. His ears twitched, hardened into cones that twisted in a semicircle as he gazed in the same direction. A forefoot pawed the ground.

Where was Aikens?

Likely he was riding a large loop and would descend back on the trail some yards behind Cord. That's what Cord would do if it were him, he thought.

Or he could be edging closer, using the pines for cover.

Cord knew he could not wait where he was. Once he left the cover of the spruce, he would be out in the open, an easy target.

He rode past the game path into a thicket of brush, with juniper and spruce trees blocking his advance, and dismounted among the trees bristling with green spines.

He ground-tied Windmill to a juniper and slipped his Winchester '73 from its sheath. He patted his horse on the neck and walked upslope, away from the clump of trees and thick brush.

He jacked a cartridge into the firing chamber of his rifle and set the hammer to half cock.

He stopped and listened to the silence. It was a silence as deep as any ocean and it surrounded him.

The tracks of Aikens were easy to pick up. He followed them into the timber. The man was riding slow and the tracks led ever higher, away from the game trail.

There was no need to follow them now.

Cord walked straight ahead, certain that he would pick up the tracks as Aikens rode back down to the game trail. That would cut time and distance from his stalking of the man who meant to kill him.

Aikens was a backshooter, like other very cowardly gun-
nies Cord had run across.

Cord stepped carefully, avoiding branches that would
crack or pinecones that would crunch.

Then he heard it.

A soft sound, perhaps a hundred yards ahead of him.

The unmistakable crack of a branch under a horse's iron
shoe.

Cord went into a crouch and headed toward the sound.

As he got closer to where the horse had stepped on that
dry branch, Cord stiffened at the sound of metal. Upslope.
Somewhere. A shell sliding into a firing chamber, a hammer
cocking, a lever being seated.

Aikens had outwitted him. For just a fraction of a second.

Cord hugged a tree just as he heard the explosion some
yards upslope from him. Then the whine of a bullet and the
rip of bark as the projectile sheared off part of the pine tree
at head height.

Splintered bark stung Cord's face.

He heard Aikens cock the rifle again.

In the silence, the sound was like the opening of an iron
tomb.

TWO

Lester Aikens kept turning in his saddle and had been looking down their back trail for the past hour or so.

"What's eatin' you, Les?" Larry Dolan asked when Lester's jitters were getting on his own nerves.

"It's that Wild Gun," Lester said, his eyes shining with a malevolent glint.

"What in hell you talkin' about?" Larry asked. He looked back down the trail. "I don't see nothin'. What wild gun?"

"That's what they call him in town. His name's Wild and he is some kind of damned vigilante or maybe a bounty hunter. I seen him a coupla times. He looks like he eats iron for breakfast and drinks blood out of a Judson boot."

"Aw, Lester. You talkin' 'bout Cordwainer. He ain't no bounty hunter. He's just another hired gun for some of the ranchers."

"It's that glint in his eyes. I know 'em when I see 'em. He ain't no ordinary hired gun."

"You think he's a-follerin' us?"

"Somebody sure as hell is. Look at them horses we brung. They're nervous as long-tailed cats in a room full of rockin' chairs."

"Pshaw, Lester. I don't see nobody back there and I been lookin' almost as much as you."

Larry was a short, thin man with a sharp-pointed nose and eyes set too close together so that, at times, he seemed cross-eyed. He was thin as a rail, but all sinew and muscle.

Lester had a small paunch, and his upper lip dripped with a scraggly moustache. He claimed it strained his food and caught skeeters at night. He was a rawboned man, nearly six foot in his smelly socks, and wore a dirty bandanna around his thick neck. He had large eyes that he kept half-hooded when he was about to kill a man.

His eyelids were at half-mast now.

"A man gets a feelin'," Aikens said. "Maybe it's instinct. Second sight. But I got a feeling that Wild Gun is gettin' real close."

"Well, we could maybe find a hidey-hole and wait for him to show up. Then blow him out of the saddle."

"Nope. I figger Wild's too smart for that. I got a better idea."

"What's that?" Dolan asked.

"One of us could double back and . . ."

"Not me," Larry said. "I want to get these horses to the 2Bar2 and draw my pay."

"If Wild is on our track, we won't neither of us get back to the 2Bar2."

"You go, then," Dolan said.

"I'm thinkin' to do just that," Aikens said.

"Go on, then. I'll meet you down at the creek when I water the horses."

"Trail goes down yonder," Aikens said. "Just past that big old spruce tree."

"Yep, it does. You goin' to double back?"

"I'll get up into the timber and backtrack, see if can dry-gulch that Wild Gun."

"Good luck, Lester."

They rode to the blue spruce and parted company without words. Dolan headed down the game path while Aikens rode up to his left, into the timber.

Lester waited until Dolan was well out of sight. Then he spurred his horse to climb the slope and rode into the heavy timber below the high ridge.

He was a man who could smell danger. He knew, deep down, that Wild was on their track, and that was that. He knew he had such instincts. They had kept him alive a good long while. He aimed to keep it that way.

He picked his way carefully through the timber, the game path below him within sight, within range of his rifle. His pistol, too, if need be. He stopped every few feet to listen. He looked up and down the trail.

Presently, he stopped again. This time he heard something. A soft sound from somewhere behind him, not in front.

Unexpected.

He dismounted and drew his rifle from his scabbard.

He waited and listened. More sounds. Furtive sounds. The trail below was empty.

Had Wild been closer than he thought?

Where was he?

He listened for hoofbeats. He heard none. Just that same soft sound. Like a man walking through the timber.

His heart began to pump faster. He took up a position behind a thick pine tree. He held on to the horse's reins with his left hand. He looked over his back trail. He saw nothing but pine boughs and tree trunks, thick brush, a juniper, and some small spruce trees.

His pulse pounded steady and strong in his ears.

Aikens let loose of the reins and levered a shell into the firing chamber of his Winchester. Then he slapped his horse on the rump. The horse headed downward toward the vacant trail.

Wild appeared out of the timber as Aikens's horse scampered downward. The horse made a lot of noise. And Wild looked at the horse, the empty saddle.

Then Aikens's pursuer disappeared for a second or two as Aikens put the stock of his rifle against his shoulder and took aim.

He saw Wild head for a pine tree.

He squeezed the trigger of his rifle and the butt bucked against his shoulder. Bark flew off the tree just inches from where Wild had been.

Missed, damn it, Aikens said to himself soundlessly.

Then he heard nothing but silence. He jacked another shell into the chamber and looked for his target.

Wild was still behind the tree. But Aikens was ready for any sign of him. His rifle was in his grip, nestled against his shoulder. He lined up the front blade with the rear buckhorn sight and waited.

He was sure of himself now.

He had the advantage.

If Wild showed any part of his body, Aikens had it covered. He was a patient man.

His eyes were hooded. He could sense death a few yards away.

Wild was pinned tight against that tree.

In a sense, he was Aikens's prisoner.

It was only a matter of time before Wild showed himself.

And when he did, he was a dead man.

Aikens waited, his pulse steady, his eyes glittering like a diamondback's.

His finger was snug against the trigger of his rifle.

One tick was all it would take.

One little tug of his forefinger.

One tick of a clock.

THREE

Cord spit out the mashed lump of rhubarb in his mouth. Deerflies swarmed to the shredded remains of the stalk on the ground. Their bluish gray bodies glinted in the sun and their diaphanous wings zizzed like sizzling bacon in the fry pan.

He held his rifle upright in front of his body and his back hugged the tree.

His quarry had reloaded and was waiting for him to show himself.

He knew he was in a bad spot, but as long as he stayed behind the tree he would shed no blood. His mind riffled through thoughts of possible solutions to his predicament. As each solution materialized, he rejected it.

He could not outwait Aikens. The man could sneak farther upslope, if he was careful enough, and find Cord exposed. One shot might be all it would take to put out his lamp.

Cord could not attempt a similar tactic. Once he left the safety of the tree, he would be out in the open for at least a second or two. Long enough for Aikens to squeeze the trigger and dust him off.

How long did it take a man to fire a round and reload? One or two seconds, at least. Would that be long enough for Cord to step away from the tree and catch Aikens in the open, aim, and shoot back?

Cord didn't know.

Aikens was an experienced killer. A dead shot, with several notches on his gunstock.

It was a gamble. But what was the risk?

His life, he thought.

Still, Cord knew he had to do something. This kind of a standoff was, in itself, a gamble. And Aikens held all the aces in his hand. Four aces against a busted straight.

Cord reached up and lifted his hat from his head, careful to hold his arm close to his body. He slid the hat down to the muzzle of his rifle. It was a dusty Stetson with a wet sweatband. It lay cocked atop the barrel of his Winchester.

He was cocked and loaded. And he had a trick up his sleeve against the four aces.

Not a royal flush, but a filled straight perhaps.

He would have a second, maybe two, after Aikens fired to step out, aim, and fire himself.

One or two breaths away from death.

More of a chance than Aikens's previous victims had had, Cord reasoned.

How trigger-happy was Aikens? Would he fall for the trick, the crude ruse? There was only one way to find out, and Cord went over his tactics. He played the game before he got to the playing field. That was the way champions did it.

That's what Cord did.

Aikens's horse crashed through the last fringe of brush and reached the game trail. The horse snorted and pawed the ground with its left front hoof. Then it lifted its head and looked up at its master. It whinnied and then was silent. It stood there on the trail, hipshot, one left foot cocked, the toe of its hoof braced against the ground.

When Cord was satisfied, he drew in a deep breath, held it, then shoved the rifle barrel with his hat hanging on the muzzle straight out, just past the tree trunk.

Almost instantly, he heard the crack of Aikens's rifle.

The bullet plowed through air with a whooshing sound and ripped into Cord's hat. It went straight through and caromed off a rock with a whistling whine.

Cord crouched, stepped away from the tree, and turned to face Aikens.

His barrel dropped and came level just below his hip. He aimed with dead reckoning as Aikens swore and took his rifle away from his shoulder. Aikens grabbed the lever and was about to pull it down when Cord's rifle exploded. The Winchester belched smoke and sparks and the rifle cracked and echoed its whiplike report off the mountainsides.

Cord heard the bullet smack into flesh, then stepped back to the tree and cocked his rifle again just as he heard his bullet smack into flesh.

Aikens let out a grunt and his hand slipped from the lever as pain shot through his body in a rush of muscle contractions and screaming nerve endings.

He doubled over as the bullet ripped through his abdomen and smashed a cup-sized hole out his back. His brain flashed with pain signals and he expelled air from his mouth in a guttural grunt. The timber spun in a dizzying swirl of green pine and spruce needles. The ground threatened to rush up to him and topple him backward.

He staggered a half step and stood up, fighting against the pain that surged through his innards. He smelled the contents of his large intestine as it split in a blood-soaked mass of tissue and muscle.

He let the butt of his rifle strike the ground and he leaned on the barrel, using the weapon as a cane. Then his mind fuzzed over and he felt a dizziness assail his senses.

His legs turned to mush and it seemed that his knees no longer locked in place to hold him erect. He slumped down, braced by his legs, and his rifle fell from his hand. He clawed for his pistol as Cord approached.

"You might think a second or two before you draw that pistol," Cord said.

"Damn your hide," Aikens growled.

His fingers wrapped around the butt of his pistol, but he struggled to tighten them or draw his weapon. Blood spurted from his abdomen and he showed signs of weakening.

Cord kept his rifle aimed at Aikens as he strode ever closer to him.

"You gutshot me, Wild."

"You were out to bushwhack me."

"Who says?" Aikens's voice was turning to a wheezing whisper as he tugged on the butt of his pistol.

"I do," Cord said. "That pistol clears your holster, you won't have time to pray before you die."

"Go to hell," Aikens spat. There was a trace of blood in his spittle.

Cord's finger wrapped around the trigger of his rifle. It would take only a flick of his finger to blow off Aikens's head. He was less than thirty feet away now, still closing the distance.

The pistol began to slide upward from Aikens's holster. Another inch and the gun would clear it.

"I warned you, mister," Cord said.

The pistol slid from the holster. Just barely. Aikens started to raise the barrel to point it at Cord.

Cord squeezed the trigger of his rifle from ten feet away. The barrel jumped when the powder exploded. Smoke and sparks spewed from the barrel.

The bullet slammed into Aikens's chest and sprouted a crimson flower on his shirt. His eyes widened for a moment and his gun hand went slack. The pistol fell from Aikens's grip as he reached up to the hole in his chest.

Blood spurted out and his eyes glazed over with a deathly frost. A gobbet of blood bubbled from his mouth as he crumpled into a heap and pitched forward, his eyes fixed.

"Too bad," Cord said as he stood over the heap that had once been Aikens. "You might have lived another five minutes."

He ejected the hull from his rifle and set the hammer to half cock.

Cord took no satisfaction in killing Aikens. He just felt empty inside, as if a deep hole had opened up somewhere in the region of his stomach. But he shed no tears for the man who had dry-gulched him. The man deserved to die and he had made the choice to end it quicker than he had to that day.

Cord walked away from the corpse and down the slope toward the outlaw's horse. He spoke to the animal, then picked up both reins.

The horse whickered softly as Cord stepped out along the game trail.

"Be all right, boy," Cord said. "I'll find you another home by and by."

His horse was waiting for him.

And there was still one more horse thief to catch left on his list of things to do that day.

He mounted up and led Aikens's horse alongside as he started down the game trail toward the creek.

One man and four stolen horses.

That one could not make good time and the day was still young enough for Cord to catch up with him.

He hoped it would not take too long. He was on the verge of tiring in the thin mountain air. He saw a hawk fly over and trail its wrinkled shadow through the trees until it vanished from sight.

Like me, he thought, the hawk is still hunting.

FOUR

Larry Dolan heard the gunshots from a distance. He stiffened in the saddle and instinctively turned to look back up into the phalanxes of timber higher on the slope he had descended. He was tempted to smile, since he had faith in Lester Aikens. But he suppressed the smile because, in truth, he really did not know whether Wild was now wolf meat or if he would have to elude Wild.

There was a long period of silence and then he heard another shot, the crack of a rifle. Just one shot. It could mean anything. A steel wire tautened in his brain, and along it ran electrical charges of doubt that surged through his head.

He wondered what that last shot meant. Was it Lester putting a last bullet into Wild's head? Or had Wild killed off Aikens?

Doubt flooded his mind and it was the not knowing that made his senses tingle. Not knowing. He spurred his horse down the trail toward the creek. Distance was now his friend, no matter what the outcome of a duel in the timber might be.

The horses could smell water and they nickered and tossed their heads as he drew closer to the creek. Once he forded it, he could ride down to the flat and have a clear look at his back trail. And he would be ready if Wild had been the victor and was coming after him.

His nerves were taut and his horse was chomping at the bit to get to the water. Those he had stolen were tugging on the lead ropes, and it took all his strength to hold them in check with the single strand that connected to all of their halters.

"Steady, boy," he said to his horse, and gave him his head.

Below, he saw the shining waters of the creek. They shimmered in the sunlight, wavelets shot with silver, a bellowing of dark water that rippled and changed shape and color as the creek surged toward lower ground.

Dolan looked back over his shoulder. He was not overly worried. He still had a trick or two left. He was just sorry Aikens was not with him, because they had planned all this perfectly, long before they had stolen the horses from the JB Ranch.

He reached the creek and found the ford he and Aikens had previously scouted. It was on a bend where the creek widened and streamed over pebbles that he could see beneath the water. It was shallow there and fairly good footing. He let the horses drink, then urged them on to the opposite bank. He made a sharp left turn into a maze of arroyos and rode over rocky ground, the remnants of an ancient moraine. He kept looking back at his tracks. They were wet for a while, then, as the horses shook off the water from the creek, his tracks were dry and invisible.

He rode over a wide plain that was almost pure shale and flint. This had been a place where the Cheyenne and

Arapaho had gathered much of their flint for their arrow-heads and hatchets.

Again, he left no tracks since he moved slowly and picked a careful path across the flat.

Beyond the plain there were arroyos spreading out in several directions, like the spokes on a wagon wheel. His eyes sought out the small blazes he and Aikens had made previously to guide them through the maze. Weathering had dulled the slashes in the aspens so that they were barely noticeable. He smiled.

They had thought this out, he and Aikens, and had made several forays into the foothills to find just the right place in case they had to elude a posse or a tracker. They had worked hard to build a pole corral in a small box canyon where they could store stolen horses and hide in ambush, just in case.

He passed several arroyos with traces of water that had run to the creek after every rain and snowmelt in the spring. The Cheyenne and Arapaho had left traces of their hunting camps in many of the arroyos, and he and Aikens had found whitened bones of deer and elk, along with broken flint arrowheads and other signs of temporary habitation.

He rode over loose talus from the limestone outcrop-pings, through a defile bordered by rugged hills, limestone bluffs, and signs of ancient flash floods. It was a wild and baffling place for anyone not familiar with that part of the Rockies.

He listened intently for any signs of pursuit, but heard nothing but the caw of crows and the peeps of chipmunks, the rustle of leaves in the gentle breeze that blew through the small canyon. The horses' hooves clacked on the talus. Any-one following him would make the same sound, and such a sound carried far up and down the corridor where he rode.

Finally, he turned left again, back toward the higher

mountains, and crossed the creek. Then he made a right turn
where he saw a blaze high on an aspen tree and continued
into the small box canyon. He and Aikens had built the
corral just inside it at a narrow aperture where boulders had
rolled down over past centuries and created two walls. The
gate was simple and it was open.

He ran the stolen horses into the small corral, then dismounted outside and picked up poles that made a crude gate
across the entrance. There was grass inside and a small con-
cave rock that was filled with rainwater. The horses could
stay there for days and survive. When he took the rope off
their halters, they all bowed their necks and began to nibble
on the tall grasses that flourished all over that box canyon.

Satisfied, Dolan rode around the entrance to the box canyon and up one of its side slopes. There, in a copse of fir and
spruce, was a place he had picked for himself. It concealed
him and gave him a good view of the terrain below, the
entrance to the small canyon.

He dismounted, ground-tied his horse to a scrub pine,
and pulled his rifle from its scabbard, along with a box half-
full of cartridges. He stuck those in his pocket and sat on a
flat rock between a pair of spruce trees that joined branches
just behind him.

He pulled a blade of grass from the ground and put the
buried end in his mouth, rinsed away the dirt with saliva, and
spit it out. Then he chewed on the sweet stalk and looked down
the long canyon. He could see for a good five hundred yards.

And this was the only way in and the only way out of the
canyon labyrinth. He smiled in satisfaction.

If Wild came after him, Dolan had a bullet in his rifle
with Wild's name on it.

Perfect.

FIVE

Cord noticed that Aikens's horse was well-fed and well-behaved. He would need him later when he packed the outlaw's body out of the timber, collected his rifle and pistol.

For now, his plan was to secure the horse near water and grass, then get on with his business. As far as he knew, there was only one horse thief left to track down, Larry Dolan. If Cord had to follow him all the way to the 2Bar2, he was determined to get those valuable horses back to their rightful owner. Come hell or high water.

The horses both smelled the creek water. Their rubbery nostrils gobbled the air and their ears stiffened as Cord descended the game trail. He patted Windmill's neck. His horse was thirsty, too. There were streaks of sweat striping his shoulders. The sun and the high altitude took moisture out of man and horse on such a day.

He saw the shining waters of the creek and had to hold

Aikens's horse in check when it bunched up its muscles, ready to bolt toward the water. Windmill snorted and whickered, but held fast under the pressure of the bit in its mouth.

He reached the creek and let the horses drink while he scanned the ground for Dolan's spoor. And there it was, five sets of hoofmarks on the path that led along the creek on his side.

He knew the man was looking for a ford. The water was swift where he was, since the creek was bordered by high banks and they kept the stream narrow.

When the horses had slaked their thirst, Cord rode away from the creek looking for a spot where he could use Aikens's rope to tie up his horse on good grass and give him access to creek water. He found such a spot in a grove of aspen a few yards down the creek. There was a low point in the bank where deer and elk had left a jumble of cuneiform tracks when they had come there to drink.

Cord dismounted and took Aikens's lariat off the saddle, looped it through the horse's bridle, and secured the bitter end to an aspen. He left the saddle and saddlebags on the horse, patted its withers, and climbed up on Windmill. Aikens's horse whinnied at them as they rode off, heading upstream.

Cord was tempted to dig out another stalk of rhubarb and chew on it, but he stifled the urge. Those horse tracks were still fresh and he didn't want anything to distract him. Somewhere upstream, there was a shallow ford, and that was likely where Dolan would cross and perhaps head out of the hills and onto the prairie.

This part of the Medicine Bows was unknown country to Cord. It was wild and rugged, with jumbled hills all around him that seemed to have sprung up in the canyon. Steep bluffs loomed in the distance, their bases piled high with talus rubble, as if stones had been dislodged in some ancient earthquake.

The tracks told a different story. Dolan was not headed for the flat, but followed the stream. Cord came upon another crossing and the tracks showed that Dolan had gone back to the other side. Why? Cord was puzzled. The man he trailed defied all logic. He should have lit a shuck for the 2Bar2, but instead, he seemed to be headed for even more rugged country in the opposite direction.

Dolan had something up his sleeve, that was certain, Cord thought as he recrossed the creek and followed the tracks until they faded out on rocky ground. He traversed a wide moraine. Cracked, broken, scrambled rocks bore the traces of sprinkled water from the horses' hooves and legs. He followed that track until there wasn't a trace of spoor. The water droplets had disappeared.

This made the tracking even more of a challenge, since he had to strain his eyes to look for overturned rocks where a hoof had dislodged a stone. He looked for those rocks that had dark undersides, signs that they had been settled in dirt and had been rolled over.

One thing was in Cord's favor. Dolan knew where he was headed, and so far, he was traveling in a more or less straight line toward what looked to be a veritable hall of mirrors. Only there were no mirrors, just a series of arroyos that jutted onto the moraine like island peninsulas.

The terrain bore strong evidence of former flash floods and violent cataclysms. Farther along, he encountered shale with flint and sandstone slabs that made the tracking even more difficult. He had to lean over so that he was close to the ground to find any chunk of shale or flint that had been disturbed or overturned. And there were not many since the stones were mostly flat and only the thinnest would break under the pressure of a horse's hoof.

Cord stopped and gazed ahead.

There were all those small breaks in the hills, each one a small canyon. Dolan could be hiding in any one of them. A queasy feeling roiled Cord's stomach as he looked over the landscape in front of him. He scanned the tops of the hills but saw only scrub pine and thick brush. He felt exposed, vulnerable to a rifle shot from any one of the small trees or bushes as he passed through them.

He rode to one side of the road, no longer looking down for tracks.

Wherever Dolan was headed, it was straight through that eerie canyon to a place he knew about. A safe haven, perhaps, a place suitable for putting up the horses and lying in ambush.

Cord was even more wary now as he ventured on. He wondered what kind of place Dolan had chosen to either make a stand or shake off any pursuit.

Earthquakes must have created this canyon of small hills, shallow arroyos, and rock-strewn gullies. It was unlike any place in the mountains Cord had ever been.

He reined Windmill to a halt.

He looked long and hard in the direction he was heading. He looked around at the small hills that jutted out from the higher mountains, the bluffs. A thought came to him as he sat there in the silence of early afternoon.

An old Cheyenne he had met said something to him once that stuck with him. The man was called Silver Wolf in the English tongue. He was a wise old bird whom Cord had met at Fort Laramie a few years ago.

"The wandering hills," Silver Wolf had said one day when they were riding through some foothills.

"What do you mean?" Cord had asked.

"The hills, the mountains. They are alive. They move."

"They don't move," Cord had said.

"Yes, they move. They wander. When you live in the mountains, you know this. Everything is alive. Rocks, trees, grass. They think. They grow. They move."

Cord could not shake Silver Wolf from his beliefs. Now, in this strange place, he knew that Silver Wolf had spoken the truth. Perhaps not in the way a white man could understand it, but these rocks, the shale, the small hills—over time, they had moved. They had wandered from their original places.

Ahead of him was more evidence of that movement. And beyond this place? What lay ahead? Nothing but trouble was his guess. An ambush. Someplace where a man could hide horses and himself. A trap.

And Cord was riding straight into it.

He gazed up beyond the small hills. There must be a way to ride above them and look down at the valley, this strange canyon.

He began to scout out a place where he could ride above the flat he was on and look both down and ahead. He rode to the nearest hill on his left and spurred Windmill to climb the slope. The hill was thick with scrub pine, scrawny juniper, and dozens of other plants and bushes. There was no path or trail through it. He gave Windmill his head and they slowly rose along the narrow ridge until they emerged on another ridge that seemed to be a spine that traversed all of the hills projecting into the canyon.

Cord breathed a small sigh of relief. Windmill shook his head. His mane flapped against his neck like some errant feathered fan. He snorted as if to clear his nostrils of dust and the memory of the climb.

Cord patted Windmill's neck and let the horse rest a few moments. Then he followed the narrow ridgeline. Every so often he looked down at the little rows of hills jutting into the canyon.

Then he saw something that seemed out of place and even stranger than the terrain he had abandoned.

There, four or five hundred yards ahead, was what appeared to be another canyon. Sunlight striped its walls with light and the fissures were strips of shadows parallel to each other.

He rode on a little farther, hunched over the saddle horn to present a smaller silhouette. He saw the back wall of the canyon and knew that it ended there.

A box canyon.

On either side were more hills, large round hills, thick with trees. The one on his right was higher than the other, and more thickly forested.

A good place for a man to hide and have an uncluttered view of the entrance to the box canyon.

The hill on the left was not high enough or close enough for Cord to look down into the box canyon.

He cursed under his breath. But, he thought, there was another way. He knew, however, that he had ridden far enough along that narrow spine above the little hills.

He looked down to his left where the ridge dropped off. Ahead, he saw a depression below the ridgeline. It was surrounded by small pines, blue spruce, and a fir tree or two. A perfect place to harbor Windmill while Cord walked ahead on foot.

He rode the side hill down to the small gully and dismounted when he was at its center. He ground-tied Windmill to a stunted juniper bush and slipped his rifle from its sheath.

Then he climbed back up to the ridge and, hunched over,

walked along it at a slow pace. He watched where he stepped
and made no sound.

He reached a point where the box canyon began and saw
that there was grass growing high in it. He lowered himself
to the ground and crawled to the edge of the ridge. He set
his rifle alongside him and looked at the opposite hill. He
saw no movement, no sign of life. Mountain breezes rustled
the limbs of the trees, and they were thick atop its rounded top.

He drew a breath and held it.

Then, on a hunch, he put two fingers in his mouth and
blew a long, loud whistle. He waited as the seconds ticked by.

A horse nickered from somewhere in the box canyon.

One of Jesse Barnes's stolen horses, no doubt, he thought.

He listened hard and heard the sounds of horses moving
around. They were faint sounds, but unmistakable.

The horses were down in that box canyon. He knew it
for sure now.

But where was Dolan?

He looked long at the entrance to the canyon. Was he
expecting Dolan to walk out in full view and look around?
No, not really. He just wanted to make sure Dolan was not
with the horses. He imagined that the horses were either
tied up or in some kind of corral.

The entrance was empty. Nothing and no one came out.

Then, as if in answer to an unspoken prayer, Cord saw
something on the opposite hill. It was just a fleeting thing,
something he might have only imagined.

A faint and fleeting glint of sunlight. Not on rock or bark,
but on metal.

Someone, probably Dolan, was on that hill, hiding in the
trees. He had not imagined it. The sun had struck the blued
barrel of a rifle when the man in hiding had moved it.

Cord held his breath and stared hard at the spot where he had seen that glint of sunlight.

A man could only stay in one position for so long. Then he would have to shift his weight and change his position slightly.

Cord waited, snug against the ground.

Move, you sonofabitch, he said silently to himself.

His hand slid to the stock of his rifle and he laid his arm up the length of the barrel so that sunlight would not strike it.

The noises in the canyon faded away and it was quiet. The silence of the mountains rose up around Cord.

The seconds dragged into minutes, the minutes into a slice of eternity that was almost beyond mortal comprehension.

SIX

The piercing whistle startled Dolan. Then the neighing of one of the stolen horses froze his blood.

What was that? he wondered. A marmot? Some kind of bird?

Or a man?

His bones stiffened and the hairs on the back of his neck vibrated and rose from his skin. He looked down at the entrance to the box canyon. There was nobody there. No sign of anyone nearby.

Just one whistle, but it was so unexpected that he had not marked its source. He looked over at the hill on the other side of the canyon, scanned it slowly for any sign of movement.

Prairie dog? Not likely, he thought. Not this high. Not in these foothills.

Something had whistled, though. Or someone.

He cursed under his breath and stared around in a 180-degree arc. Nothing moved. Nothing made a sound. His palms began to sweat. He wiped one hand on his trousers. He could hear the skin rubbing against the cloth.

Nothing wrong with his ears. He had heard that sharp, short whistle and it had unnerved him.

Where in hell was that Wild Gun?

Dolan shifted his weight on the rock. His buttocks were going numb. His rifle moved slightly, away from him, and he eased it back closer to his body, behind the branches that concealed him.

He listened intently for any sound, animal or human. He listened for a hoofbeat, a branch rustling against another, a scratch, a clink of stone, a cough, a grunt, or an animal scurrying among the pinecones and needles.

Nothing but silence. An eerie, unnatural silence at that.

Across the way, on the other hill, Cord continued to stare at that same spot where he had seen a glint of sunlight. He knew that there was someone there, sitting or standing, amid the copse of trees. Sooner or later, he reasoned, whoever was there would have to move. Bones and flesh tired after a time of immobility.

Cord waited, his arm still covering his rifle, his chin hugging the ground. It would take only a second to slide his rifle into position for a shot.

He was ready. Every fiber in his body was ready. And he was comfortable lying flat on the ground behind some bushes that did not block his view of the other hill.

He might get off only one shot. And it had to count.

He gauged the distance, thought about the trajectory of the bullet from his rifle. The empty space between the hills made a difference. The pull of gravity was farther away from most of the distance the bullet would travel. Yet his sights were dead-on. He had sighted his rifle at twenty-five yards, then tested it at one hundred yards. Dead-on.

He figured the distance from his hill to the other to be less than two hundred yards. Closer to a hundred and fifty. He looked at the entrance to the box canyon, judged the distance between the foot of each hill. Then back to the spot on the other hill. He judged his estimate to be pretty close to being accurate.

Finally, Cord's patience paid off.

He saw a single spruce branch move. The branch was low to the ground and it was the only one that swayed and bent before it sprung back to its original position.

He slid his rifle toward him and slipped the butt in the crook of his shoulder. He sighted down the barrel, straining to see what, or who, had caused that single branch to move. As he waited, and watched, more branches moved and he saw a shadowy figure of a man stand up with a rifle in his hands. The man stayed in the shelter of the spruce, but his legs, torso, and arms were visible.

The man lifted one boot and stomped the ground in front of him. That action exposed more of his body. He continued to stamp at something on the ground, and that's when Cord saw a flat rock where the man had been seated.

Cord curled his finger around the trigger of his rifle and lined up his sights. He aimed for the man's midsection and held his breath. He squeezed the trigger and the rifle bucked against his shoulder as the .30-caliber cartridge exploded in the firing chamber.

The boom and crack of the rifle split the silence wide open and the sound echoed in the surrounding hills.

The man turned slightly as Cord fired his Winchester,

and the bullet slammed into his hip. Dolan spun around and crashed backward into the trunk of the spruce. Blood sprayed from the wound and he let out a loud cry of pain.

Then Cord saw Dolan hunch over into a crouch and bring his rifle to bear on him. Smoke from Cord's rifle hung in the air for a few seconds, then began to disappear as the breeze shattered it into a white wisp.

Dolan fired his rifle.

Cord saw the spurt of orange sparks and puff of smoke before the bullet whistled over his head, clipping branches from the bushes before it landed in the dirt behind him.

Dolan was in plain sight, but he was hunched over so that he did not present a clear target.

Cord saw him lever another cartridge into his rifle's firing chamber. That's when Cord took the second shot. He aimed, once again, toward the largest part of Dolan's body and squeezed the trigger. Then he rolled to his left and jacked another bullet into the chamber of his rifle.

Dolan screamed in pain as the bullet seared his right thigh and crunched through spruce branches. It was a shallow wound but gouged out a chunk of flesh, and the wound spewed blood onto the spruce branches and the ground.

Dolan recovered and stood up as blood seeped down his right leg and into his boot.

SEVEN

Abigail Barnes stood at the front window of the ranch house. She watched as her daughter, Lelia, shooed chickens out of the front yard with a straw broom. The chickens squawked and ran from her. Others took flight and cleared the picket fence. Feathers floated in the air. The chickens continued to squawk in protest. Abigail frowned.

"Chickens loose again," Abigail's husband, Jesse, said from his place at the dining room table. He sipped the last of his coffee, his plate marked with the tracings of fried eggs, ham rinds, and hominy grits.

Abigail didn't answer right away. She stared at the foothills where she saw movement beyond the hayfield that bordered the grassy pastures.

She was a corpulent woman with pudgy lips, a large button nose with a mole on its tip, close-set porcine eyes, and a neck that was encircled with excess flab. She had sturdy legs and muscular arms and wore her gray-streaked hair in a bun.

"Somebody's comin'," she said to Jesse. "Out of the hills, I reckon."

"Who?" Jesse asked.

"Dunno. But looks like maybe one man and a bunch of horses."

"Cord Wild," he said.

"Can't tell."

Lelia opened the gate and chased some of the chickens around the side of the house toward the chicken coop out back. But she stopped and looked toward the hills herself and shaded her eyes for a better view.

It was still early morning and the sun was just edging up over the horizon. The pastures were tinged with pink and the mountains were still shadowy monuments with only their snowcapped peaks shining brilliant under long gray clouds that were slowly turning to gold.

Lelia's fair skin was berry brown from the sun. She had long black hair that shone even in that hazy morning light with the sheen of a crow's wing. Her black eyes were almond shaped, almost Asian, and her lips were voluptuous, as if she had dipped them in some acidic wine. Her patrician nose gave her face a look of Grecian symmetry and her lithe body was as finely curved and contoured as a Venetian vase. Her faded dress clung to her body like a furled sail. She clutched the broom with dainty, delicate hands that matched her small feet and trim ankles.

In a word, she was a beauty.

Her heart began to beat as she saw the lone rider leading six horses. The other horses were fanned out behind him, but he was unmistakable.

It was Cordwainer Wild.

"Ma," she called as she turned to the window.

Her mother nodded in acknowledgment and turned away from the window, a silent growl on the puffy face.

"Unless I'm mistaken, that is your wild man a-comin'," she said. "I s'pose he'll want me to fix him some breakfast this time of day."

"Likely he's been chewin' on rhubarb." Jesse stood up and carried his cup to the window.

"I see six horses," he said, "'sides his own Windmill."

"Them the horses what was stolen?" Abigail said in a snorting tone.

"Yep, maybe. Three mares and my best stud, Gladiator."

"Why you'd hire a lout like that to go after them horse thieves is beyond me," Abigail said.

"He ain't no lout, Abbie," Jesse said.

"He ain't nothin' but a drifter with a gun. You should hear what they say about him in Cheyenne, Jess."

"Abbie, I ain't got the least idea what they say about Cordwainer in town."

"They say he's just a gunslinger. When the law or some shop owner gets in trouble, they say they'll get the Wild Gun."

"Well?"

"That tells you who he is, Jess."

"Well, he's right handy with a six-shooter, that's for sure. That don't make him bad."

"No? He who lives by the gun dies by the gun, I say."

"He got my horses back, didn't he?"

Jesse watched as Cord got closer. He saw the lumps on the two saddled horses and guessed they were the bodies of the horse thieves. Abigail wouldn't like that much, he thought. He sipped the last of his coffee and walked back to the table, set the cup down.

"I'm goin' out to meet up with Cord."

THE WILD GUN 37

Abigail walked to the window and harrumphed when she saw the bodies of the two men tied to their saddles.

"Looks like he got more than your horses," she said. "'Less I'm mistaken, he's done kilt two more men."

"In a fair fight, I reckon."

"Pshaw, Jess. He probably shot 'em both in the back."

"That's not Cord's way."

"No, he probably likes to see men suffer afore he kills 'em."

"You don't know the man, Abbie."

"I know the type of man he is," she said.

Jesse walked out the door. He was tired of arguing with his critical wife. She could peck a man to death with that sharp tongue of hers.

Lelia chased more chickens around the house and disappeared as Jesse walked to the gate. He held up a hand in greeting as Cord rode up. Then he slid a hand into his front trouser pocket and pulled out a wad of folded greenbacks.

"Howdy, Cord. You got 'em."

Cord reined up. He pushed his hat back from his forehead and looked at Jesse.

"Got your horses and the two who stole 'em, Jess. I leave them all in your good hands."

"What am I supposed to do with two dead outlaws?"

"Your call, Jess. If I were you, I'd send 'em back to the 2Bar2 and let Horace Weatherall read the handwriting on the wall."

"I don't trust that man," Jesse said.

"Well, he likes your horses an awful lot."

"He's a thievin' scoundrel and I wouldn't put it past him to come after me just to draw my blood."

"That's a possibility, all right," Cord said. He dismounted as one of the ranch hands, Pat Varnum, walked over from a corral in front of the barn. He was a lanky, short man,

bowlegged as a pair of parentheses, with a scruffy moustache, face and hands tanned and weathered by sun. He wore
a crumpled hat with a Montana crimp and smoked a quirly
that stuck tight to his lower lip.

"See you got your horses back, Jess," Pat said. "They look
to be in fine shape."

Pat looked at Cord, nodded. "Wild," he said in acknowledgment.

"Varnum," Cord said.

"Got them two horse thieves, too, did ya? How come you
brung 'em here?"

"Evidence," Cord said.

"Huh?" Varnum scratched the back of his head.

"Proof," Cord said.

"Hell, you should have just let them two rot out up in the
hills," Varnum said.

"To each his own," Cord said and swung down out of the
saddle.

"Take my horses to the stables, Pat," Barnes said. "Curry
and grain 'em. See that they drink some of that springwater."

"Yes, sir," Pat said. He took the lead rope from Cord,
blew smoke out of the side of his mouth.

"And put out that quirly, Pat, less'n you set somethin'
afire when you do your chores."

Varnum threw his cigarette down and ground it under
his boot heel.

"What about them?" Pat asked, gesturing toward the two
dead men. "And their horses?"

"I'll have Ray tote 'em over to the 2Bar2 when I see him,"
Jesse said.

"We could sell them horses and saddles," Pat said. He
started walking toward the livery, pulling on the lead rope.

"You want to dig graves for those two, Pat?" Jesse said. "They're gettin' right ripe."

"Naw. You do what you want with 'em."

Cord wrapped his reins around the hitch rail and reached into his saddlebag. He pulled out some butcher paper, unwrapped it, and filched a stalk of rhubarb from the stack inside. He stuck the stalk in his mouth and chewed the end of it.

"Hungry? Want some grub, Cord?" Jesse asked.

"No, I chawed on jerky and hardtack a while back, Jess. I just wanted to let you know I'm not doin' this anymore."

"Here's your money, Cord. Twenty a head. They's eighty dollars in this here wad." He pressed the money into Cord's hand.

"Thanks," Cord said.

"What do you mean you ain't doin' this no more?"

"No more man tracking, killing. I've had enough of this sort of work."

Lelia came around the corner of the fence and ran up close to Cord.

"Howdy, Lelia," he said. He took off his hat out of politeness.

"Why, howdy, Cordwainer," she said. "You got our horses back."

"Yes'm," he said. He took the rhubarb out of his mouth and stood awkwardly, so close to her he could smell the lilac water on her face, the fragrance of her hair.

Jesse looked on with the air of a proud father.

"Did you get hurt?" she asked.

Cord shook his head. "No'm," he said.

"But you got them two horse thieves. I can smell 'em."

"Yes'm, they been dead awhile."

She looked up at him with frank admiration. Her eyes fluttered and her lashes were coquettish. Deliberately.

Cord squirmed in his skin.

"How about some coffee?" she asked. "And you can tell us all about how you hunted them men down and . . ."

"He don't want no coffee, Lelia," Jesse said.

"I could use a taste," Cord said in contradiction.

"Why, I'll see if we have a fresh pot. Daddy, you comin'?" She flitted away like some prairie nymph through the gate and into the house.

"Sure you want coffee, Cord?" Jesse asked.

Cord slid the bills into his trouser pocket. "And to set a spell," he said.

"Lelia overstepped her boundary," Jesse said.

"She's the prettiest thing I've seen all week," Cord said.

"Abbie won't like it none, you and Lelia battin' eyes at each other."

"Abigail doesn't like much of anything," Cord said and then wished he hadn't.

"Well, she's all I got to keep the house in order."

"I know. She won't have to worry about me. I'm not looking for a wife just yet."

"No, maybe you ain't, but Lelia, she's got eyes for you. Plain as day."

"I wouldn't know," Cord said.

"I hope you don't find out, then."

"You object to me courtin' your daughter, Jess?" Cord asked as the two headed for the front door of the ranch house.

"I ain't objectin' so much, but Abbie, she . . ."

Cord held up a hand to stop him from saying more. "I know, I know," he said. "Abigail thinks I'm riffraff, a no-good saddle tramp with a trigger-happy disposition."

Jesse laughed. "That's pretty much what she thinks, all right."

"I'll try not to spill coffee on her doilies," Cord said as they reached the door.

The two men went silent as they entered the house, both prepared to face the hostility they would find inside. In the form of Abigail.

But all Cord could think about was Lelia. Women like her didn't come down the pike that often. She was a beauty, all right, but maybe not for the likes of him.

Or was she?

A man could dream, couldn't he?

EIGHT

Lelia whispered something to her mother when Cord walked into the house.

Abigail frowned but waddled off to the kitchen to fetch the coffeepot. Lelia began to empty the tray in her hands. She set cups at three places as her father commandeered the chair at the head of the table.

"Set yourself, Cord," Barnes said, pointing to the chair next to him.

Lelia sat down as her mother approached with a steaming coffeepot in her hand.

"Ma'am," Cord said as he removed his hat and nodded to Abigail.

"Mr. Wild," Abbie said. "I see you brought back my husband's horses."

"Yes'm," Cord said as he sat in his designated chair.

"And two dead men who stink to high heaven," Abigail said.

Barnes shot Cord a sharp look as if to stay his tongue.

Cord said nothing. He just nodded as Lelia looked on, smiling at Cord.

Abigail poured coffee into the cups as if she were doling out fare for the poor.

Barnes sat there like a lord, with his wide shoulders and heavy frame, his brushy moustache and thick gray-streaked eyebrows on ledges over his hazel eyes. He hailed from Tennessee, where he had cultivated a love of horses since early boyhood. He had met Abigail in church and she immediately set her hooks out for him. Before he knew it, she had wormed her way into his father's household, taken charge when Jesse's mother had died. She kept him away from other eligible girls until his father forced him to marry the woman who doted on him. Abigail had been slim when they married, but ten years of indulgent eating had put pounds on her small frame. Abigail had gained what she wanted—Jesse—and no longer cared about her personal appearance. She possessed him, and Lelia had sealed the marriage contract, until Jesse felt as if he was Abigail's prisoner in a loveless marriage.

His thick arms braced his muscular torso on the table as he glowered at his wife, who filled his cup at the very last. She sat down after placing the coffeepot on a round piece of earthenware in the center of the table.

"Well, here we all are," Lelia said with a joyous lilt to her voice. She lifted her cup and batted her eyelashes at Cord.

"You should not speak unless spoken to, Lelia," Abigail said to her daughter.

"We don't get company that often, Ma," Lelia said.

"It's good to be with real people again," Cord said. He smiled at Lelia.

"What do you mean by that, Mr. Wild?" Abbie said.

"I come out of the mountains with only horses for company," Cord said.

"And two corpses," Abbie said. "Men you shot dead."

"Abbie . . . ," Barnes warned.

"You're right, ma'am," Cord said. "Two horse thieves who should have been hanged. According to the law, that is."

"What do you know about the law, Mr. Wild?"

"I know the punishment for horse thieves, ma'am," Cord said.

"Now, now," Barnes interrupted, "let's not talk about dead men and the law. Abbie, show some politeness to our guest. He's not on trial here."

Cord drank from his cup as if to escape the tirade he was sure Abigail was ready to unleash on her husband.

"He's your guest, Jess, not mine," Abbie said.

"Ma . . ." Lelia put a hand on her mother's as if to shut her up before they were all embarrassed. At the same time, she slipped her foot out of her sandal and stretched her leg. She touched Cord's leg with her toes and wriggled them.

Cord looked across the table at Lelia as he felt something on his leg. She wore a look of innocence. But her toes wiggled and she began to stroke his leg up and down with those same soft toes.

Then she smiled coquettishly at Cord.

His face was a mask as he continued to stare at Lelia.

"Is something wrong, Mr. Wild?" Abigail asked as she noticed a trickle of sweat crawl from under his scalp and stream down to his cheek. "Is it too warm in here for you?"

"No, I'm fine, ma'am," Cord said. He wiped his cheek. "It must be the hot coffee."

Just then, there was a knock on the door.

"Come in," Jesse called.

The door opened and a man walked into the front room. He removed his hat when he saw the assemblage at the table.

"I see you got your horses back, Jess," the man said.

"Pull up a chair, Ray," Barnes said. He pointed to a chair pushed against the wall, next to another, set there for extra company.

"Ray Dobbs, meet Cordwainer Wild," Jesse said as Ray lifted the chair and brought it to the table.

"Heard of you," Ray said, extending one hand to shake Cord's.

"Likewise," Cord said. "You're Jess's foreman."

"Yep." Ray sat down in the chair, dropped his hat to the floor.

"Coffee, Ray?" Abbie said with an exaggerated sweetness to her tone. This was an indication to Cord that Ray was welcome at her table while Cord was not.

"No'm. I'm plumb full of java. I just wanted to know what Jesse wanted to do about them two corpses out there. They're right ripe already and the sunrise ain't goin' to make it any better."

"Cord thinks you ought to ride them thieves back to the 2Bar2 and let them bury the carcasses," Jesse said.

Ray looked at Cord.

Ray was a short, lean man, wiry as a willow sapling, wearing a dusty shirt, a bandanna around his neck, and a silver and turquoise band on his left wrist. He had short sandy hair that sprouted in all directions, with a gleam of sweat where his hatband had left an impression on his hatchet forehead. He had pale blue eyes that looked almost white at certain angles.

"You can take their rifles and gun belts, boots, saddles, bridles, anything else you want, and tote 'em over to the 2Bar2 bareback," Cord said.

"You don't want none of their stuff?" Ray asked.

Cord shook his head.

"Well, we can always use an extry saddle or two, and the guns might come in handy down the road," Ray said. He grinned a gap-toothed smile.

Lelia withdrew her foot and slipped it back into her sandal.

Cord let out a sigh of relief.

"I'll lug them dead boys over to the 2Bar2," Ray said, "but Weatherall will throw a prime fit when he sees them boys dead."

"They're his responsibility," Jesse said. "Horace hired 'em, he can damn sure bury 'em. Take as many men as you need, Ray, and just run them horses through Weatherall's gate and then hightail it back to the JB."

"Yes, sir. I'll take Ned Parsons and Boyd Cummins along in case we run into any nervous hands on the 2Bar2."

"Good idea," Jesse said.

Ray rose from his chair and grabbed the wooden back to return it to the wall. "I'll get right on it, boss," he said. "Pleased to have met you, Wild."

"Call me Cord."

"Okay, Cord."

Ray set the chair against the wall, then walked back, picked up his hat from the floor.

"Mrs. Abbie, Miss Lelia, thanks for your hospitality," Ray said. He walked toward the front door.

"Anytime, Ray," Abigail said. "You're always welcome in my home. Unlike some people." She shot Cord a look of scorn.

Ray walked outside and eased the door shut behind him.

"Cord's a guest here, too," Jesse said to his wife.

"Your guest. Not mine."

"I tell you, woman, sometimes you raise my gall to an intolerable level."

Abigail got up without finishing her coffee. "You're known by the company you keep, Jesse," she said, and strode off toward the kitchen under the glare of Jesse's eyes.

"Sorry, Cord. The woman has a mind of her own."

"I can see I've worn out what little welcome I had. I'm going to Cheyenne for a shave and a warm bath."

Cord started to rise up from his chair.

"Cord, I may need you again," Jesse said. "If Weatherall comes gunnin' for me."

"I told you, I'm going to hang up my gun except for hunting and snakes," Cord said.

"Must you leave so soon, Cord?" Lelia asked, a pleading tone to her voice.

"Yes'm," he said. "I'm plumb weary and about as ripe as those dead men out there."

"But you'll be back?" she said.

He looked at her, and something inside him melted. Quivered. He stood up, hat in hand.

"I might come to call sometime, if it's okay with your folks," he said. His tone was soft and full of an unspoken promise.

"It's sure all right with me," Jesse said, a smile on his face.

There was a loud "Harrumph" from the kitchen, followed by the slam of a cupboard door.

"Well, that's one of you," Cord said to Barnes. "I'll be seein' you, then. Lelia, Jesse."

Lelia watched Cord walk to the door, open it, and go out. Her face fell and she looked as if she might cry.

Jesse reached over and patted the back of her hand with his.

"Don't you worry none, honey," he said. "Cord'll be back. One of these days."

"I hope so, Pa," she said.

Then she rose from her chair and skipped to the window. She watched Cord mount up and ride away. His departure left her with a feeling of sadness that surprised her. There was something about the man that touched her deeply. He seemed so strong in contrast to the other men she knew from town and on the ranch.

Then there was her mother. Cold of heart and stern of mind.

"Good-bye, Cord," she murmured to herself. "Please come back."

Jesse finished his coffee as he stared at his daughter. Unless he was mistaken, she had her sights set on Cordwainer Wild. If so, she might wind up with a broken heart.

For, he knew, Cord was not only a man not easily tamed, but one who might not live long. He knew Cord would not hang up his guns for long.

NINE

H orace Weatherall cocked his pistol, a Colt .45, jammed the snout behind the horse's ear, and squeezed the trigger.

The explosion shattered the silence of the afternoon. The horse's head jerked as the bullet entered its brain and churned it to pulp. The hind legs spasmed and the horse stopped moving.

Smoke spewed from the barrel of Horace's pistol and the acrid sting crept into his hairy nostrils.

The two men with him nodded as the horse stopped moving.

"That was only a scratch on his leg, boss," one of the men said. "It might have healed up, given time and some salve."

"The horse was lame, Jimmy," Horace said to James Rowan, the man who had spoken. "I won't have cripples on the 2Bar2. Man or beast."

Jimmy hung his head. There was a sheepish cast to his face.

Horace holstered his pistol.

"That's the last of the blue roans," Corwin said.

Horace removed his hat and smoothed his heavily pomaded hair at both temples. He worried his lower lip as he looked at the corpse of the roan.

"And I wanted to breed that mare," Horace said. "Dumb as she was."

The men around him exchanged glances. None of them really understood Horace. He had several horse breeds on his ranch, but he seemed to want more variety. The man had inherited money, but most of the men who worked for him thought he was some kind of eccentric fool.

His pastures were full of colorful horses: Appaloosas, duns, sorrels, bays, pintos. He was always crossbreeding, but most of his experiments were failures. If he didn't like a foal's appearance, he was apt to destroy it before it reached yearling status.

And he sent men to far-flung ranches in Colorado and Wyoming to steal horses whenever he was dissatisfied with the breeds and horseflesh offered at local auctions.

There was something just not right with Horace, according to men who had been with him for four or five years. He seemed to be obsessed with something, but none of them could figure out what his obsession was, exactly.

"Rider comin'," Jimmy said as he looked off toward the distant gate of the 2Bar2 spread.

"Visitors?" Horace said as he put his hat back over his glistening hair.

"Just one," Jimmy said. "And he looks like he's been rid hard and put away wet."

The approaching rider's horse was lathered with sweat

rolls that were yellowish and puffy. Streamers of the lather flew off the horse like buttery tassels.

"Don't recognize either horse or rider," Horace said.

"Me, neither," Jimmy said, his eyes squinted to narrow slits.

"Watch him real close, Jimmy," Horace whispered from the side of his mouth.

The rider slowed his horse and stared down at the two men.

"You Horace?" the rider asked.

"One of us is," Horace said. "Who's askin'?"

"My name is Jessup. Bart Jessup, and I'm in a heap of trouble."

"We don't have no aid station here," Horace said. "Little sympathy, neither."

"You don't understand. I've rid all the way from Joplin, Missouri, to give you a message. But I got a man on my tail what's been tryin' to shoot me outen the saddle."

"Joplin? A fur piece," Horace said.

"I got a message from your brother, Abner. It's real important."

"Light down, son," Horace said. "I ain't seen my brother in two or three years."

Jessup slid out of the saddle and landed off-balance. His legs were wobbly and his shirt and trousers were stained with sweat. He gasped for a full breath and blinked red-rimmed eyes.

He was a short-statured man and his face was stippled with at least three days' worth of beard stubble. There was a wild-eyed look about him that was tinged with fear.

"Abner, he's a-comin' with thirty head of prime Missouri Trotters. He stole 'em from some old man in Missouri, name of Wild."

"Wild, you say?" Horace asked, suddenly on full alert to the stranger's message.

"Yep. Lucas Wild, whose boy is hot on my track, far as I know."

"There's a man named Wild here in Wyoming," Horace said. "I think his Christian handle is Cordwainer."

"Kin to the boy who's hell-bent on snuffin' out my candle," Jessup said. "Boy's name is Earl Wild and he's plumb crazy."

"You better tell me all you know, Jessup," Horace said. "I ain't never heard of either the old man or his son Earl. But the Wild what's here in Wyoming is a big old thorn in my side."

Jessup turned his head to look over his back trail. His hands began to shake and more sweat leaked from under his hat brim.

"They call this Cordwainer the Wild Gun," Jimmy interjected. "He goes after a man, the man ends up dead."

"I don't know about him," Jessup said, "but that kid brother of his is a hothead and come near to putting my lamp out once't or twice."

"Why is this kid so bent on killing you, Jessup?" Horace asked.

Jessup took off his hat and wiped the back of his hand across his brow. He blinked as sweat dripped into his eyes and stung them.

"When we went to capture them horses, the old man tried to stop us. Abner got mad as hell and roped him. He drug old man Wild for a good quarter mile, and then Wild's woman come tearin' outen the house with a scattergun and let off a load of buckshot that must've stung Abner somethin' fierce 'cause he got even madder. He rode up on the woman and knocked the Greener outen her hands and then plumb put the boots to her right then and there."

"Abner raped the woman?" Horace asked.

"He started it. Eddie Lomax hopped on her, too, and so did Freddie Calkins. Woman was screamin' her fool head off and must've brung the kid out of the barn. The kid came runnin' up with a pitchfork in his hand, cussin' like a dock worker on the Mississip', and Abner had to waylay him with the butt of that scattergun to shut him up. We all lit a shuck after that and I was ridin' drag when I seen this Wild kid comin' after us on horseback, hell-bent for leather."

Jessup paused and looked over his shoulder again as if expecting Earl Wild to come riding over the horizon.

"Then what happened?" Jimmy blurted out suddenly.

"Abner waved me away and took another trail to keep the kid from getting back any of them horses we stole."

"And the kid follered you?" Horace asked.

"He sure as hell did and fired off a shot that whistled over my head like an angry hornet. I ducked and put the spurs to my horse and hauled ass as far away from the horse herd as I could get. Lost track of Abner and the others, and the kid started to gain on me."

"How'd you manage to outdistance him, Jessup?" Horace asked.

"I got into them Oklahoma hills and lost him for a time, but he outfoxed me and caught up by the time I got to the Wyoming border. I tell you, that kid's plumb determined to put me six feet under."

"Did he say anything to you?" Horace asked.

"Yeah, he said plenty," Jessup replied. "He said him and his brother would hunt me down to the ends of the earth and make me die slow and hard. He scared the livin' hell out of me, I tell ya."

"Well, we can take care of that boy for you," Horace said.

Just then, Jimmy looked up and saw a rider coming from the direction of the Weatherall ranch house.

"That's Harley Davis," Jimmy said to Horace, "and he looks like bad news."

Horace cursed under his breath and turned to see what brought Davis out.

Davis rode up, his face drawn and head hanging down as if in shame.

"I got bad news, boss," he said. "Real bad news."

"Spill it," Horace said, a look of annoyance on his now florid face.

"Aikens and Dolan are dead and they must've lost them horses they stole 'cause they come back strapped to their own mounts 'thouten them."

"What?" Horace exclaimed.

"Both shot dead and stripped of their gun belts. Mighty sad."

"That's all?" Horace said. "No sign of who killed my boys?"

"Nope. Them horses just come back home with their bodies tied to their bare backs. Like a message."

Horace cursed and looked at Jessup as if to blame him for the death of his men.

Jessup swallowed in bewilderment.

"The Wild Gun," Jimmy murmured.

But Horace heard him and set his jaw as his eyes blazed with the fiery light of hatred. Then he turned to Jessup.

"How far behind you is my brother? And does he still have them horses?"

"I dunno," Jessup said. "After tryin' to escape that kid, Earl, I lost a lot of time in Oklahoma. They can't be more'n a day or so behind me. But they're drivin' some thirty head and only got three men to wrangle the herd."

"Good enough," Horace said. "I know Abner, and when he makes up his mind to do a thing, he don't stop till it's done."

"What about that kid on my tail?" Jessup asked. He held his hands together to halt the tremors.

"I don't see no sign of him. He might be callin' on his

brother about now." Horace looked off into the distant horizon as if looking for dust or a rider.

"That means we'll have two of them Wilds 'stead of one," Jimmy said.

"We'll be ready for 'em by the time Abner gets here," Horace said.

"Wild is a manhunter, Horace. He don't just ride up out in the open. He's sneaky as grease in a fryin' pan. I doubt Dolan and Aikens even saw him comin'."

"Oh, they saw Wild, all right," Horace said. "He was probably the last thing they saw, the dumb bastards. And I was countin' on gettin' them horses in my stable."

"We better keep our eyes peeled real sharp," Jimmy said.

"Yeah," Horace mused as he drew in a heavy breath. "I want that man dead, and I'm going to put a bounty of one hundred dollars on his head for the man who takes him down."

"What about that brother of his?" Jessup asked.

"Him, too," Horace said. "Same bounty. We can't make no headway with any Wild Gun still breathin'."

"Fair enough," Jimmy said. "I'll make sure everybody's on the lookout for either feller."

Jessup breathed a long sigh of relief. He had come to the right man. The Wild brothers were as good as dead. Horace was even more formidable than Abner, and that gave Jessup confidence that he would escape death at the hands of Earl Wild.

That look in Horace's eyes told him all he wanted to know.

TEN

As always, Cord took notice of his surroundings and of the people on the streets in Cheyenne. He felt a weariness that was not born of fatigue, but of some nagging sensation of failure. He had killed two men, and the responsibility of taking their lives weighed heavily on his heart.

Yes, the men had been horse thieves, and yes, they had meant to kill him.

But they were only acting on orders from someone else: Horace Weatherall, a greedy, thieving, and conniving man. He was the one who should have paid the price. Paid with his life.

As Cord rode down Main Street, he looked at the faces of the people he passed. The wan complexions of the chubby-faced women, the gaunt, tired looks on the faces of drifters, and the set jaws of cowhands and wranglers. The merchants looked grim and determined as they looked out their doorways, and the Mexicans driving burro carts looked as if they were on some religious pilgrimage, their brown eyes alight with anticipation and fervor as they sought places to display their goods: clay vessels and hand-woven rugs, trinkets fashioned of silver and turquoise.

Cheyenne was thriving, but Cord could not help thinking of the desperation on the faces of many as they walked to and from their destinations.

He did not linger in town, but rode toward the mountains where he lived, bone-weary and troubled with the weight of the lives he had taken with his gun.

He had meant it when he told Jesse Barnes that he would track no more horse thieves.

"A man makes his own society," Cord had told him. "And I don't want to live a life with blood on my hands."

"But you're good at what you do, Wild," Barnes had said. "Nobody but you could have gotten my horses back."

"The cost is too high," Cord told him. "Those men I killed were only used as tools, like hammers or branding irons. The man who should have paid the price was Horace Weatherall."

"So?"

"Unless I catch him red-handed stealing a horse, I couldn't take him down without breaking the law."

"The law is clear on that point, Cord."

"No law is clear, Jesse. They're all muddied with something. And I don't wear a badge."

"No, but I'm thinking we might form some kind of organization that could appoint you as an official regulator or maybe a peacemaker."

"Peacemaker? Hardly."

"A regulator, then," Barnes said.

"You mean a bounty hunter."

"If you want to call it that. You'd be doing a big service to the other ranchers in the territory."

"I'm no man to take on the task of chasing after horse thieves."

"Why not?"

"Not in my nature. As I said, a man creates his own society. I don't want to go into one where I deal only with lawbreakers. If I did, I would run for sheriff."

"Not a bad idea, but the sheriff in Cheyenne has very limited powers. As a regulator, you'd have free rein to go after horse thieves."

Cord shook his head.

"Free rein to act as judge and jury. Free rein to take another man's life without a jury trial or legal judgment."

"That's one way of looking at it."

"That's the only way, Jesse. Once you take a man's life, he is gone forever. With no second chance. No chance for redemption or forgiveness."

"You know what your trouble is, Cord?"

"I've told you some of it."

"You got too much of a conscience. You think too much about what a man might be rather than what a man is."

"Maybe so. But if I have a conscience, it's mine to deal with, same as life."

Cord left town, with its rattling carts, bustle, and grasping commercial hands, and entered the foothills where he followed a dim game path that was barely visible through the rocks and brush that blanketed the fissure he rode through.

Still, he noticed that the ground had been disturbed slightly. There were fresh horseshoe tracks, and when he examined them more closely, he felt an electric tug of recognition.

He knew those tracks, for he had seen them before, in another time and place.

His ride took him up a circuitous path, into the timber, where the scent of pine, spruce, and balsam wafted to his nostrils under a light mountain breeze. His heart quickened as he approached the place where his hidden cabin lay nestled along an old prospector's creek.

The cabin was sturdy, made of debarked logs by an old prospector named Barney Crumb. Cord had known him and visited him often when he first came into the territory.

Barney froze to death during the previous winter after he injured himself with an axe and could cut no more firewood. At the time, Cord's younger brother, Earl, had come out from Missouri and was with Cord when they found Barney, frozen to death, in the spring. They buried the man and Cord moved in. Earl stayed with him for a week, then returned home.

Cord had not seen his brother since that time.

Now, as he rode up to the cabin, he heard a horse snort.

Earl was sitting on a stump in front of the cabin, slumped over, dozing. His horse was ground-tied to a small juniper bush a few feet away.

Cord rode up, dismounted, walked over to his brother, and placed a hand on his shoulder. He shook the boy awake, and Earl looked up at him with swollen eyes and a grimy face.

"Cord," Earl said. His voice was weak and Cord sensed the weariness in his voice.

"Hello, little brother," Cord said and hunkered down next to the boy.

"You look plumb tuckered, Earl," Cord said. He helped his brother to stand and led him into the cabin. The boy was on shaky legs and Cord had to hold him tight to keep him from collapsing in Cord's arms.

Inside, it was quiet and there was the smell of ashes in the fireplace, the musty smell of weathered logs, and the faint musk of wood and cooking grease from the small kitchen. They sat on a wooden couch that was padded with bear and elk hide. Earl's eyes fluttered as he lay back and stared up at his brother.

"You look starved, Earl," Cord said.

"I am," Earl said. His lips were dry and cracked. He seemed to have grown some since Cord had last seen him. When he swept away Earl's hat, he saw a clump of tousled brown hair that was clogged with dust and grit.

"I've got plenty of grub. What brings you out here? Everything all right at home?"

Earl crumpled over and buried his head in his hands. He began to cry. His sobs filled the room with anguished bubbles of sound that tore at Cord's heart.

"He—he's dead, Cord. Pa's dead, and he died so horribly."

Cord felt as if he had been stabbed in the chest and gut. He shook his head in disbelief and denial.

"So, you tracked one of them to Cheyenne?" Cord asked when his brother had finished relating the horrible details of the murder of their father and the rape of their mother.

"Yep. He was the only one a-runnin', and God knows where the others are. But they got our horses and I figured they were headin' this away," Earl said.

"You guessed right, Earl. Abner's brother has a ranch north of Cheyenne. And he's cut from the same bolt of cloth as his brother. They're both horse thieves."

"They got to pay," Earl said. "What they did to our pa and ma."

"Oh, they'll pay, all right," Cord said.

"How you figure to get them, Cord?"

"It'll take some doing. Horace Weatherall is surrounded by a bunch of dry-gulchers and backshooters. It won't be easy."

"They got to pay," Earl said again.

"And they will. It's going to take some planning and maybe some tricky stalking."

"I'll help you," Earl said.

Cord patted his brother on the shoulder.

This news changed everything for him. He wanted to give up the life he had been leading, but circumstances now prevented that. He would have to rely on his wits and his gun. He knew he could not rely on the law to help him. The reach of the sheriff in Cheyenne was only within city limits, and it would take time and patience to hunt down a U.S. marshal.

No, this was something Cord had to do himself. He wasn't sure about his brother. Earl was still just a kid, still wet behind the ears and much younger than Cord. He was a good shot, but not wise in the ways of men. Especially men with guns. Maybe it was best to keep his brother out of it and just go it alone.

It would not be easy to get at Horace Weatherall. But, from what Earl had told him, Abner was even more vicious and heartless than his older brother.

Then, too, there were the stolen horses. Thirty head. Horace would alter the brands and probably try to sell them to the army or to a private rancher.

And how many men did Horace have on his ranch? Cord did not know.

He had taken two of them down, but he knew there were more. And these were men who shot to kill and didn't ask any questions.

A tentative plan formed in Cord's mind.

The only way he could get at Horace and his brother Abner was to hunt down their cohorts one by one until only those two were left.

It would take much planning and perhaps more than a little subterfuge.

And, he thought, he would have to be almost invisible.

A tall order, he reasoned.

There was a lot of prairie in Wyoming, and men with sharp eyes would be on the lookout for him.

"You'd best stay out of this fight from now on, Earl. I can handle it."

Cord rose from the couch and looked down at his brother.

"I want to kill them. Every damned one of them. With my bare hands." Earl was not begging, but demanding.

Cord shook his head.

"I can't bring you into this, Earl," he said. "It's just too dangerous. I'll try and get our horses back and get you some wranglers to drive them back home. But you're worth more to me than those men who killed our pa."

Earl started to cry again. He whimpered and squeezed the side of his head with both hands. Tears leaked from his tortured eyes and Cord could not look at him.

He loved his brother, but he knew he was right to keep him out of harm's way.

Better to have a broken heart, he thought, than lose a brother to a more experienced gunman.

He walked into the kitchen and looked for something to fix for Earl that would fill his stomach and take his mind off revenge.

He thought of their pa and choked up as he pulled a basket of hens' eggs from the cupboard and took down a skillet from the wall. There was bacon and potatoes he could fry up and they would eat together.

From the other room, he heard the sound of Earl's sobbing and it was all he could do not to cry himself.

ELEVEN

When Horace saw the dead bodies of the two men Cord had killed, he erupted in a blind rage that terrified his other men.

And to see that they had been stripped of saddles, rifles, and gun belts drove him to the edge of normal rationality and sanity.

He stood with several of his men in front of his house, a framed structure of whip-sawed boards and a sloping shingle roof. The two dead men were still tied to their horses and had begun to ripen in the sun.

The ranch house was nestled in the foothills, tucked back into a natural horseshoe formed by low hills. Behind it, the mountains rose up in ascending phalanxes. The land itself was gently rolling prairie and jutted up against the Barnes ranch. Horace had a thousand acres but had always wanted more, and he'd had his eye on the JB spread for some time.

Now he saw a way to get it, with all its assets, and he was determined to take the property by force.

"We may not get the Wild Gun right away," Horace said to his men, "but we can damned sure go after the man who hired him: Jesse Barnes. Besides that, I want all of Barnes's horses. I'm plumb tired of messing around with a few head here and a few head there. I want Barnes wiped out."

"You mean kill him?" Jimmy asked.

"Kill him plumb dead," Horace said with a savage tone to his voice.

"It ain't goin' to be no easy thing," Rowan said. "He's got a sharpshooter or two on his payroll."

"I got a plan," Horace said. "I think it might work."

The men gathered around Horace as he told them how to lure Barnes out into the open and dry-gulch him.

"We steal a couple or more of his horses in the dead of night," Horace explained. "But we don't run 'em to my ranch or into the mountains. Instead, we leave plain tracks and lead him into that gully what's washed out twixt his ranch and mine. You know the place."

The men nodded. They all knew about that place. It was almost a ravine, a deep depression caused by centuries of flash flooding next to a small mesa that rose above the fissure. It was clogged with brush and rocks, and many a cowhand and wrangler had ventured there to recapture strayed cattle and horses. For some reason, a lot of animals used the gully as a hiding place, a refuge, and it was crawling with rattlesnakes and other critters that made the place almost inaccessible on horseback.

"Danged good idea," Jimmy said, which brought him a lot of scornful looks from the others.

"Think he'll fall for it?" Will Corwin said. "Barnes, I mean."

"If he wants his horses back, I'm betting he will," Horace said.

"When do we do this?" Corwin asked.

"Tonight," Horace said. "There's no time to waste. Besides, I think if we drop Barnes, the Wild Gun will come out of his hidey-hole and try to mix in."

"Wild don't foller no regular trail, boss," Rowan said. "He's real sneaky."

"We'll make sure that news of Barnes's death gets into Cheyenne and draws that rascal out."

"Wild don't leave no tracks," Jimmy said. "We've tried to find out where he bunks down, and so far, he can't be found nowhere."

"You let me worry about Wild. He's just one man and we've got bigger fish to fry."

The men stared at Horace, as puzzled as ever about his behavior and demeanor. Jimmy was gape-mouthed, but knew better than to question his boss any further about Wild or the plan Horace had laid out for them.

"I just want two men for this night job," Horace said. "Two men who won't fail. Any volunteers?"

Jimmy Rowan was the first to raise his hand.

"I reckon that's in my line of work," he cracked.

Will Corwin also raised his hand. A lanky wisp of a man who was all muscle and sinew, having worked on building a railroad when he was young. Rowan was beefy but hard-muscled with a face leathered by the sun, except for his forehead, which was covered by a crumpled felt hat that looked as if it had been mangled by cougars, then patched with thick thread in several places.

All the men wore gun belts studded with .45 or .44 cartridges, and all owned at least one rifle; some had two or three.

Horace looked up then and scanned the sky. To the north, he saw the large white clouds building. They were blowing down from the mountains, topping the snowy peaks, and billowing over the valleys. It was a hot day and the sun was sucking up moisture from the creeks in the valleys.

"The weather is on our side," Horace said. "It's going to rain this afternoon. That will make the ground soft when you ride over to the JB. You'll leave clear tracks that Barnes can easily follow."

The other men looked at the mountain sky. They all saw the clouds blowing toward them and knew they would be over the prairie by early afternoon.

"A good sign," Jimmy said.

"A damned good sign," Horace agreed. "It would even help if the rain lasted into the night."

"And let up by the time we run them horses out to the gully," Corwin said. He spat out a stream of tobacco juice from a wad he had in his mouth.

"Don't push it," Horace said. "With them winds behind 'em, them clouds will pass over pretty quick once they dump their rain."

All of the men grunted in agreement. They had seen prairie storms before. They were sometimes fierce, but they moved fast. The clouds would turn black and fly lower in the sky and dump a lot of rain, gully washers, in a short time. And the men all had slickers to keep them dry.

"Looks good," Corwin said.

"You boys bury these men," Horace said. "And get ready for some delicate work tonight."

"Where do you want 'em buried?" Jimmy asked, a look of dumbness on his face.

"Bury 'em right in front of that gully," Horace said. "That

way, Barnes will have to ride over 'em when he chases down his stolen horses."

The men all laughed at the irony and rightness of Horace's order.

"That'll learn him," Corwin said with a wry chuckle.

"Damned right," Rowan said.

Jimmy and two other men began to lead the horses away toward the far gully while two others walked off toward one of the barns to get shovels. Horace watched them go and felt a sense of pride in his men.

They didn't need much instruction. They knew what to do. He paid them well and treated them fair.

This was a trait he and Abner had learned from their father, who had taught them both all the tricks of his trade—which was horse stealing and dry-gulching.

Lemuel Weatherall had started stealing horses as a boy, and when he married and had two sons, he was pretty well off, financially. He had taught the boys to shoot rifles and pistols, how to handle and build a lariat. All the tricks of his trade.

They had lived in the Missouri Ozarks, and through the war, they had all been guerrilla fighters, picking off Union troops that ravaged the countryside.

The hills of the Ozarks made for good hiding places, and the Weatheralls were experts at covering their tracks and leading Union scouts into dangerous ambushes.

Unfortunately, Lemuel made a mistake. He stole several horses from a judge in Harrison, Arkansas, and was caught red-handed.

The boys watched their father when he was hanged in the courthouse square.

Their mother never recovered from Lemuel's death and wasted away until she died of heartbreak, leaving the boys orphans who needed to ply their father's trade with even more caution.

"Why pay money for something when you can get it for free?" their pa always told them before they went on a raid to obtain horses.

The boys had honored their father's memory by becoming even more adept at stealing horses.

Horace had set his sights on the West, where he knew there were even more horses to be had. He no longer had the hills, but he had the mountains, where he could hide horses and men from the law.

And until Wild had come into the picture, he had done very well.

Wild was like a shadow.

He had seemingly come from nowhere, and the ranchers had hired him to do their killing. So he was no more than a hired gun, but he was no pilgrim. The man was a tracker, and he was relentless. More than one horse thief had fallen to his gun. Wild had gained a reputation, almost overnight. Other horse thieves had left the territory because of him, or had just stopped their nefarious activities.

And the ranchers had put a sobriquet on the man. They called him the Wild Gun. And when someone's horses were stolen, the ranchers called for the Wild Gun to aid them.

Horace had only been the latest to encounter the shadowy man who had now killed two of his men.

Such a man could not be allowed to continue in his pursuit of horse thieves.

Even as he walked back into his house, Horace was thinking of a way to draw Wild into the open and kill him.

Perhaps, he thought, taking Barnes down would do the trick.

It was almost certain that someone on the JB Ranch,

Barnes's wife or daughter, would send for Wild to avenge the death and retrieve the stolen horses.

In fact, Horace was counting on it.

Even a shadow could not escape a strong light. And Horace meant to shine a blazing torch on Cordwainer Wild.

TWELVE

Earl and his brother ate together. By the time Cord had washed the dishes and put away all the plates and flatware, Earl was asleep on the couch, his gun belt hung on the arm of the divan. The boy did not hear the thunder that boomed in the late afternoon, nor awake to the patter of heavy rain on the roof.

Cord went to bed, his thoughts swirling with memories of his dead father, a man he had admired and respected. He did not think about revenge or retribution, but about his dear mother, all alone now, deprived of any source of income since most of their horses had been stolen.

He vowed to get the horses back to Missouri.

He slept fitfully until the rain stopped, then drifted into dreams of towns and people, obstacles that arose in his path through a maze of clapboard buildings and tawdry saloons where strangers with strange weapons attacked and chased him up stairs and through rooms that led to still other rooms. And in the dream there were large black horses that flew over the prairie like huge birds without wings.

He awoke in a sweat and lay in bed until his mind cleared and the dregs of the dreams faded from memory.

It was still dark out when he arose and strapped on his gun belt to go outside and watch the sky break open at the first crack of dawn in the east. He chewed on a stalk of rhubarb and thought of his father.

Lucas Wild had instigated the rhubarb chewing.

"I call it 'ruminatin' rhubarb,'" his pa had told him. "Makes you think of other things 'sides your troubles. Try it. The stalk's got enough sting in it to make you mindful of chewin' while your mind ruminates on other things."

The habit had caught on and Cord had chewed stalks of rhubarb at times when he needed to think clearly and make difficult decisions.

After the sun came up, Cord made preparations to hunt down the men who had murdered his father and stolen thirty head of horses from the family ranch.

He figured that Abner had not yet arrived at Horace's ranch, but he had a great deal of scouting to do. And he still believed that Horace was a menace and must be brought to justice, even if it was only frontier justice, without the law's sanction.

He gathered up cartridges for his Winchester rifle, and added two boxes of .45-caliber pistol cartridges to his kit. The ammunition would be carried in one of his saddlebags. He packed hardtack and beef jerky, wrapped in oilcloth, filled two canteens, and tied his slicker behind the cantle on his horse's rump.

Earl watched all this preparation in silence, but he was fuming inside that his brother was going it alone.

Outside the cabin, the air was fresh and the ground wet. The creek was running full bore and there was a tang to the air from the still dripping trees, the pine needles, and the freshly washed spruces and firs.

Earl watched his brother pack his saddlebags and hang canteens from his saddle horn. His face bore an expression of sadness and his eyes seemed to reflect the gloom that was inside him like a dark smoldering furnace.

"I want to go with you, Cord. I need to go with you. I'll die if you don't take me with you."

Cord turned from his horse and looked at Earl.

"You won't die. You need rest. You did enough. You tracked and chased Bart Jessup all the way to where I can find him, at Weatherall's. You've done enough."

"No, I haven't. I should have killed Jessup, but I missed him every time."

"We all miss the target sometimes."

"But you didn't see what he did, what Abner and the others did to Pa and Ma."

"No, but you can't carry that with you all your life. You did what you could and now I've got to pick up where you left off."

Earl's eyes flared with anger, and he rose up from the ground where he had been sitting. He clenched his fists and walked close to Cord.

"I didn't tell you all of it, Cord," Earl growled from deep in his chest.

Cord froze.

"All of it? What do you mean?" he asked.

"That ain't all that happened. Them draggin' Pa and killin' him in cold blood."

"They left him dead, didn't they?"

"Just about. Pa died, all right, but that ain't all there is to it."

"What in hell do you mean? They raped our ma, you said. Then they left. Right?"

"They left, all right. But that ain't all that happened. It—it's hard for me to talk about it."

Cord stepped to his brother and gripped both of Earl's shoulders in his hands.

"What else?" he said, his eyes slitted, a hard cast to his jaw. "We'll get our horses back and I'll get a couple of wranglers to help you drive 'em back to the ranch in Missouri and you can go on from there."

"There ain't nothin' to go back to, Cord," Earl said, his eyes welling up with tears.

"You got Ma and the house, a barn, corrals, plenty of pasture."

"There ain't no house no more."

"What?"

"There's more that happened after they killed our pa," Earl said.

Then he bent over in a desolate crumple and began to sob. Tears streamed from his eyes and drenched his cheeks.

Cord gripped him hard and felt the pang of Earl's grief in his innards. It was as if he had been punched in the gut.

"Maybe you better get it all out, Earl," Cord said. "What else is there to tell me?"

Earl straightened up and wiped his cheeks with the back of his hand. He still sobbed, but the tears had lessened.

"While I was gettin' down my rifle to chase after Abner and the others, Ma was draggin' Pa into the house and screamin' at the top of her lungs. 'You go after those murderers, Earl,' she yelled. 'You kill ever' damned one of 'em.' I told her I was goin' after them. She kept screamin' and yellin' and I run out and got to my horse."

"Was Pa dead when Ma dragged him into the house?"

"Yeah. He wasn't breathin' and his face was all mashed up by rocks and such. His clothes were shredded and bloody. He was plumb dead, all right."

"So, then what?" Cord asked.

"I was gettin' on my horse when I heard Ma scream again. Real loud this time. I looked back at the house and I seen smoke pourin' out of the front door."

"What?" Cord exclaimed.

"I seen Ma a-huggin' Pa on the floor and the front room was blazin' with fire. I jumped off my horse and ran up to the house. I figgered to go in and drag Ma and Pa out of that room. But I saw Ma catch fire and then she sort of crumpled up and stopped screamin'. The flames by then was roarin' through the front door, the roof was smokin', and I couldn't do nothin'. I stood there, helpless as a drawnded cat, and watched the whole house burn clear to the ground."

Cord choked on something in his throat. His eyes widened in disbelief as he tried to picture the gruesome scene in his mind. It was hard to imagine his mother's last moments, consumed by fire as she embraced their dead father's body.

Yet such a scene became vivid in his mind. He knew how much their mother loved their father. She was completely devoted to him, as he was to her. She never complained, never tried to boss her husband around. She was no church mouse; she was a strong woman with strong feelings and was not afraid to speak her mind. But the love she had for their father was deep and everlasting.

Overcome by grief, she had not wanted to live without Lucas and had set the room on fire so that she could join her husband in death.

So much for his mother's strength. She obviously had not wanted to face life without Lucas and had taken her own life.

"I—I'm so sorry, Cord. It was horrible and I just couldn't

tell you what happened right off. It don't seem real, even now. But it happened."

"I know, I know," Cord said. He put his arms around Earl and hugged him tight.

"I just couldn't save Ma," Earl said, snuffling the dregs of his tears through his nose.

"No. It all happened so fast, there was no chance to save her. And she did it to herself."

"Why? Why?" Earl asked.

Cord shook his head.

"Who can explain such things? Who can say how each one of us deals with such grief? Ma didn't want to live without our pa. That's all there is to it."

"But there's nothing left. Ma and Pa are just ashes, and our house, our home, is gone."

"There's always the land, Earl. You can rebuild."

"I never want to go back there, Cord. Not with the awful memories I have of that day."

Cord stepped back and patted Earl on the shoulder.

"No, I don't imagine you would want to go back there, brother. You can just bunk with me until you finish growin' up and go out on your own."

"I need to go with you to hunt down that Weatherall bunch," Earl said. "You got to take me with you."

Cord thought about it.

His look at his brother was long and searching. He saw a very young man, still in his teens, who was broken inside, but made of sterner stuff than Cord would have imagined.

He knew that Earl came from good pioneer stock. He had all the makings of a soon-to-be man. He had already shown that he had grit and determination, that he wasn't afraid to chase after a bad man, a killer.

Maybe, Cord thought, now was the time for Earl to take

the first steps into manhood. Lord knows, Cord had started his jump at about the same age, trading horses and chasing after horse thieves when he wasn't much older.

"Can you follow orders?" Cord asked.

Earl nodded. His eyes lit up with an eagerness that came from deep inside his being.

"Do whatever I say, whenever I say it?"

"Oh, yes, yes, Cord. I'll be like a slave to whatever you tell me to do."

"We'll pack you some grub and such. I got a black slicker just like mine that you can wear when it rains. Saddle your horse."

"Oh boy," Earl exclaimed. "Thank you, thank you, Cord."

"You won't thank me when you have to lie stock-still for hours under the beating sun and have to sleep on a cold bed of rocks for a night."

"Like hell I won't," Earl said with a wide grin exposing all his front teeth.

"Get to it, then, while I go in the cabin and rustle up some more supplies. Take along plenty of ammunition for your pistol and rifle. You might have to do a passel of shooting."

Earl dashed toward his horse while Cord went back inside the cabin to gather the necessary supplies to sustain his brother on what might prove to be a long trail.

Cord hoped he was making the right decision. Earl would be exposed to much danger and might have to face more experienced men, killers who were also keen marksmen.

But if there was ever a time for Earl to grow up, now seemed that time.

Cord just hoped they would both survive, though they were outnumbered and outgunned by men just as desperate as they were.

THIRTEEN

While Cord and Earl partook of troubled sleep at Cord's cabin, Rowan and Corwin rode through the driving rain, the wind at their backs, toward the JB Ranch.

They carried freshly fashioned lariats and a solid plan to capture Barnes's best horses and lead him on a path to his death.

Horace watched the two men disappear into the veils of cascading rain and smiled with satisfaction, his face contorting through the window that coursed with streams of rainwater. A glowing oil lamp exaggerated his demonic features had anyone looked at him during those moments.

He saw his ranch expanding and the pastures filled with horses that he had not paid for. That was a satisfying thought and gave him a sense of immense power. He saw himself as some kind of monarch of the plains, commanding large numbers of men who did his bidding and eliminated all competitors.

This was a dream he had held ever since leaving Missouri and coming to the Great Plains. And now his brother, Abner, was driving more horses to his ranch, which would add to his wealth at no cost to him.

By morning, he hoped, Barnes would be dead and he would leave behind a daughter and a widow. Horace could easily drive the widow away and take over the JB Ranch.

He pulled a cigar from his vest pocket, bit off the end, and lit it. He blew smoke against the windowpane and turned away, the sound of the rain on the roof both soothing and full of promise, as if the gods were on his side and giving him the advantage he needed to move up in the world.

Rowan and Corwin rode slowly through the rain. There was no need to hurry. They would stake out the horses they would steal and wait for the rain to stop. That was their plan. If they moved fast, all of Barnes's hands would be inside, out of the rain, and they would encounter no resistance.

As it turned out, their assumptions were correct.

When the two thieves reached the JB Ranch, the rain was already beginning to lessen in intensity. They rode around checking the various corrals. They spotted three horses in a pen, mares, and knew why they were there. In another pen, some distance from that one, there was a lone horse—a stud.

"Them mares are in heat," Rowan whispered to Corwin. "Look at that there stud. He's pawin' the ground to dig a hole to get at them. Those mares are mighty valuable to Barnes."

"You bet."

"Then them's the ones we'll take. That stud horse will screech and holler, but that will bring Barnes out and he'll find the mares gone."

"Damned good idea, Jimmy," Corwin said in a soft undertone.

When the rain became a drizzle, the two men went about their task.

They rode up to the breeding pen and Will swung open the gate just wide enough to let Jimmy ride in and rope one of the mares. Then Will entered right behind and roped another one. The third mare danced away from them and they let her go out of the gate.

That way, they had to lead only two mares, but all three would be missing.

They moved fast and silently as they led the two mares away from the breeding pen and out into open pasture. They tromped through wet mud and knew the wind would blow off the water and leave deep impressions around the corrals and the breeding pen.

The stud whinnied loud and long as the mares disappeared.

Lamps came on inside the house and bunkhouse. Doors swung open. Men in slickers emerged into the darkness and ran toward the sound of the agitated stallion. Voices rose up as men made startling discoveries.

There was confusion and bewilderment among the hands on the JB.

It took more than an hour for Jesse Barnes to fully assess what had happened.

Three of his mares were missing. With a torch, he saw that they had not just escaped when the gate came open by accident.

The horses had been stolen.

And he knew in his heart who had stolen them.

Anger boiled up in him as he held the torch over the

muddy tracks as his men strode back and forth between corrals and the barn. He heard their voices as each called out the status of other horses and searched for any more missing livestock.

Finally, as he turned to go back to the house where his daughter and wife were anxiously awaiting news of what had happened, he saw two men with a horse between them.

"We found one of the mares," one of the men shouted. Jesse recognized the voice of Ned Parsons.

"We got Bessie May," the other man said. "She was behind the barn."

The two men came close with the mare, and Jesse saw that the other hand was Ernesto Rojas, a Mexican wrangler who had been with him since he'd started building his ranch.

Jesse patted Bessie May's withers. "Good job," he said. "They didn't get all three of those mares in heat."

"Looks like they just let Bessie May run free," Ned said. "Should we put her back in her pen so Big Karl can mount her today?"

"Yeah, put her back," Jesse said. "And I'm going to need two men to help me track those other two mares. Any suggestions?"

Ernesto stepped away from the mare.

"I'll go with you. And Danny is the best tracker on the ranch. A good shot, too."

"Good suggestion," Jesse said. "We'll start out at daybreak. Ernesto, go find Danny and tell him to saddle up and bring his rifle. Far as I know, only two men stole those horses and they should be easy to track on this wet ground."

"Sure thing, Jess," Ernesto said as Ned Parsons led Bessie May back into the breeding pen. She pranced and flicked her tail as she romped back into the pen. The stud snorted and whinnied in approval, his muscles flashing velvet in the firelight from Jesse's torch.

Rowan and Corwin did not linger.

They headed straight for the gully with the two stolen mares, still dripping from the rain, which had now stopped. It was still dark as pitch, but they knew the way to their destination.

They did not look back as the voices from the ranch died away in the distance.

"Old Jesse Barnes won't try and foller us until it gets light," Will Corwin said. "Right, Jimmy?"

"Nope, I reckon not. By the time the sun comes up, we'll have these mares in that gully."

"Barnes don't stand a chance," Corwin said.

"Not with men up on that long mesa," Rowan said. "I can't wait to see old Barnes dance under a hail of rifle bullets."

"It'll be a sight for sure," Corwin said.

They rode on, with the horses sloshing through small pools of rainwater, leaving tracks on the flat ground.

The wind was up on the tail of the storm and blew ripples in the standing water. The two men spoke no more as they ate up ground, moving ever farther from the JB Ranch and onto Weatherall's spread.

The wind turned chill, and the two men felt the brunt of it from the north. Fingers of wind reached into their slickers and they shivered some until they squeezed the sides of their raincoats with arms and elbows.

Black clouds blew over them and wafted away to reveal shining stars and a bulbous moon shrouded by thin scarves of dark clouds that lingered high above the earth.

There was no sign of the men up on the tabletop as the sun arose in the east and brightened the landscape with its brilliant rays. It rose beneath the black clouds and turned the lowest ones into smoky streamers that soon dissipated. The prairie seemed to glow golden in the piercing sunlight, and the gully emerged with its tangle of vegetation while the oblong mesa stood like a minor fortress above the rolling terrain.

"There she is," Will said. "Just like always."

"What in hell did you expect? That it would have washed away in last night's rain?"

"Just glad to see it is all. No need to get yourself in a hissy over it."

"I ain't in no hissy," Rowan said. "Wimmen get in hissies, not men."

Will chuckled as they led the two mares into the gully and slipped the lariats off their necks. They chased them deep into the shallow ravine and turned their horses back when the mares had disappeared.

"That ought to hold 'em," Rowan said.

"Now what? Do we ride back to the ranch or go up on the mesa?"

"We get the hell away from here, that's what we do. Horace will see to the rest of it."

"I'd still like to see old Barnes shot clean out of his saddle."

"The others can tell you about it, Will. Just tend to your own damned business."

"No need to get in a huff about it, Jimmy."

The two rode off toward the Weatherall ranch. Above them, on the mesa, men lay flat in wait, rifles at their sides, their slickers shining as they gave off steam from the rain. They were invisible from down below, shielded by rocks and brush that stippled the flat ground.

Soon, Jesse Barnes and two men appeared as tiny dots on the horizon.

Jimmy could see them coming without rising from the

ground. Just on the edge of his peripheral vision. His heart quickened and he said in a loud whisper: "Here they come, boys."

"Shut up," one of the men said, and Jimmy clamped his mouth shut.

"It's like they wanted us to track them," Danny said to Barnes. "Them horse tracks just go in a straight line right toward that gully yonder."

"Maybe they'll turn directly," Barnes said.

Ernesto stood up in the saddle to peer ahead. In the far distance he could see the entrance to the gully. His eyes scanned both sides and he tried to see if there was any movement atop the low mesa that formed one wall of the ravine.

He saw nothing.

"I do not like this," Ernesto said. "It is too quiet and I do not see nobody."

"They wouldn't run them mares into that gully, would they?" Barnes asked.

"Not unless they wanted to fool us," Danny said.

"Keep your eyes peeled," Barnes said, but he was not very suspicious right then. "Just see where the tracks go."

The three men rode up to the gully. Danny's gaze traversed the entrance. He saw where the two men had driven the mares into the wash and then, as he rode a few yards to the side, he saw that there were only two sets of tracks.

Both men on horseback had left the mares and had ridden off toward Horace Weatherall's ranch.

"There's something wrong here," Danny said. "It don't make no sense."

Barnes sat his horse and gazed into the brush-choked ravine, a look of puzzlement on his face.

"We got to go in there and get them mares out," he said.

Those were his last words.

The snouts of rifles suddenly appeared atop the mesa. There were loud explosions as each man up there fired down at Barnes.

The bullets ripped into his chest and he writhed in the saddle with the force of the lead that tore through his body. A shot to his neck brought an eruption of blood and a last throaty gasp of air.

Barnes toppled from the saddle as Danny turned his horse and headed back the way he had come.

Ernesto wheeled his horse and drew his pistol.

But he could see no target. He saw only flashes of flame and puffs of white smoke from atop the mesa.

He dashed away from the hail of lead and knew that the only man meant to die that day was his boss, Jesse Barnes.

He knew he was outnumbered and outgunned, and he jammed his spurs into his horse's flanks. The only way to survive was to put distance between him and the riflemen above him.

Danny reined up when he was well out of rifle range and waited for Ernesto to catch up to him.

"Well, that's it for Jesse," Ernesto said when he rode up. "What are we goin' to tell Abigail and Lelia?"

"You know 'em better'n I do. You tell 'em what happened."

Ernesto's face contorted into a sad bronze mask.

"It will be hard," he said. "We should have done something."

"There was nothing we could have done. Weatherall stole them mares for one purpose. He wanted to kill Jesse."

Tears welled up in Ernesto's eyes.

"I know," he said. "There was nothing we could do. You and me, we are lucky to be alive."

"You're damned right, Ernesto. It could've been us back

there, all shot up, our blood soakin' into the ground. Let's get the hell out of here."

Ernesto wept quietly on the ride back to the JB Ranch. He had lost a great friend. And now he would have to face the widow and the fatherless daughter and tell them the sad news.

The sun did not seem so bright anymore.

FOURTEEN

Cord mounted up and watched as Earl climbed into the saddle.

"Where do we start?" Earl asked.

"We'll ride up to the JB Ranch. That will be our base. I want to tell Jesse what happened to our pa and ma and have him bunk us when we're not out hunting."

"Will he help us?" Earl asked.

"I'm betting on it," Cord said and touched spurs to Windmill's flanks.

The two wound their way down the trail, headed toward Cheyenne.

Cord rode alongside his brother once they reached the flat. He reached into his pocket and pulled out a pair of rhubarb stalks. He handed one to Earl.

"Chew?" Cord said.

"Ugh. I hate rhubarb."

"Ruminatin' rhubarb, Earl."

"I know. That's what Pa always said when he chewed on those things. I hate the taste."

Cord retrieved the proffered stalk and put it back in his pocket. His teeth crunched on the one in his mouth.

"Makes the ride a lot easier," he said.

"How long will it take us to get to that ranch?" Earl asked.

"Two, maybe three hours from Cheyenne."

They passed through town with its smells and carts and people barely noticing them. Earl viewed everything with wide eyes and the curiosity of a country boy. He felt more at home on the prairie with the sky a blue canopy above and miles of lonesomeness stretched out ahead.

They entered the JB Ranch on a winding road under an archway that marked the boundary. The ranch house loomed up after they topped a rise and descended into a swale of grass.

"There it is," Cord said as he pointed an arm toward the house.

When they rode up and halted their horses at the hitch rail, Ernesto opened the front door and came out to greet them.

"Wild, you come at the right time," Ernesto said. "A bad time."

"What? Where's Jesse?"

"He is dead, Cord. It is a long and sad story."

Cord and Earl dismounted and wrapped their reins around the crosstie.

"But you're going to tell me, Ernesto."

"Yes, I will tell you."

And he told the entire story about the stolen mares, the tracking, the ambush when Jesse Barnes was murdered.

Earl listened in rapt fascination. He did not know the man who had been killed, but he drank in the entire story with his full attention.

"Abigail and Lelia are inside the house," Ernesto said. "They are weeping. They are grieving. I am happy that you are here, Cord."

"Just a little too late, it seems," Cord said. "Let's go in. I want to see Abigail and Lelia."

"But of course. Follow me." Ernesto led the way and they all entered the house.

Abigail looked up when Cord entered, her face wet with tears, her hair tangled from kneading it with frantic fingers. Lelia cowered next to her, her face just as wet, her eyes wide and tear-filled, one arm around her mother.

Cord took off his hat and stood there. Earl noticed the gesture and quickly removed his own hat.

"Abigail," Cord said, "I'm so sorry about Jesse. Words can't express my sorrow and my sympathy for you."

"Oh, Cord," Lelia exclaimed as she arose from the couch and ran to him. She clasped Cord in an embrace and laid her head against his wide chest. "I'm so glad you're here."

He patted the back of her head with gentle taps of reassurance.

She stepped back and looked up at him.

"You will get those men, won't you? And kill them."

"Yes," Abigail hissed from the couch. "Jesse deserves justice, but I know that won't bring him back to us."

"No, it won't," Cord said. "I'll see what we can do."

"Who's that with you?" Abigail asked. Lelia looked at Earl as if she had just noticed him.

"This is my brother, Earl," he said. "Horace's brother murdered our pa, stole most of our horses, and our ma died, too."

"Oh, I'm so sorry," Abigail said.

"So we came here to tell Jesse we're going after the whole bunch at Weatherall's. It's way past time that he was called up to answer for his crimes."

Abigail arose from the couch. She walked over to Cord and looked up at him. She wiped the tears from her face.

"I'm glad you're going after them, Cord. You know Jesse would be pleased if he were still alive."

"I know," he said.

Lelia hugged Cord and stood on tiptoe to plant a kiss on his cheek.

He felt the heat of her, and when he looked down at her face, he could see the passion in her eyes. She was a beautiful young woman and she aroused feelings in him that had lain dormant. This was not the time or place, but she was desirable, and who knew what might lie ahead for the two of them? It was a fleeting thought, but the thought was there. He bowed his head and replaced his hat.

"We'll be heading out now," he told Abigail, "but I might like to stay at the ranch when I'm not out hunting down Weatherall and his men."

"Of course," she said. "You can stay here in the house. With Lelia and me."

"The bunkhouse is okay," he said.

"Nonsense. I won't have you out there. You'll be more comfortable in here. Lelia and I will cook for you and see to your every need."

"That's very kind of you, Abigail," he said and turned to leave. Ernesto stood next to the door, waiting.

"Good-bye," Earl said. "Glad to have met you ladies."

He put on his hat and followed his brother and Ernesto out the door.

Cord and Earl walked to their horses.

"Are we goin' after them Weatherall hands right away?" Earl asked.

"Yep. First, we'll see about those mares. I know where that little ravine is and they might still be in there."

"I will go with you," Ernesto said.

"Just to get the mares back, Ernesto. The rest of the way, we'll go it alone."

"I understand," Ernesto said. "And I need to bring Jesse's body back. I will get my horse. He is still saddled."

"Fine," Cord said. He mounted his horse.

He and Earl did not have to wait long for Ernesto. The three rode away from the JB Ranch toward the gully that was on the Weatherall ranch, not far from the JB boundary.

Jesse's body was still there. Buzzards had been at it, and were circling in the sky. The birds had picked at Jesse's eyes and ripped his shirt open where he was the bloodiest. It was a sickening sight and Earl gagged to keep from throwing up his breakfast.

From deep inside the gully, they heard the whinny of horses.

"They're still in there," Cord said. "Ernesto, you and Earl stand guard while I ride in and see if I can drive them out."

Ernesto looked up at the mesa. It was quiet and he saw no one on top. Still, he pulled his rifle from its scabbard and scanned all around. Earl followed his lead and slipped his rifle from its boot.

"It's awful quiet," he said to Ernesto.

"It was not so quiet this morning."

Cord rode into the gully. The mares had cleared some of the brush so that he had a path to follow. He heard them crashing around, their hooves striking rock as they pawed to gain purchase on unstable ground.

A few minutes later, he spotted one of the mares. She was frantic and nickered when she saw Cord and Windmill. He rode up to her and spoke in low tones to calm her.

"We'll get you out of here, girl," he said. "Just hold on."

He approached, and the mare stood for him. He slipped his lariat around her neck, then saw the other mare, a dappled gray that was perched on a small ledge beneath the escarpment.

"Come on, girl," he said to the dappled gray, and the horse climbed down.

Cord made another loop at the bitter end of his lariat and secured it around the gray's neck. Then he held on to the center of his rope and turned Windmill back toward the entrance.

Ten minutes later, they were out of the gully. Ernesto beamed with pleasure.

"If you will help me," he said to Earl, "I will put the body of Jesse on my horse and tie him down."

Earl slid his rifle back into its leather sheath and dismounted.

"Take the feet," Ernesto said.

Earl lifted Jesse's boots while Ernesto tugged at the dead man's shoulders and lifted him from the bloody ground. They draped Jesse's body on the rump of Ernesto's horse, just behind the cantle. Ernesto ran a rope underneath his horse and wrapped it around Jesse's hands and stiffened ankles, tied it tight.

"I will take the horses back and we will bury Jesse," Ernesto said.

"Thanks, Ernesto," Cord said. "You ride careful."

"I will. *Vaya con Dios, amigo,*" he said in Spanish. "Go with God."

Cord watched Ernesto ride back toward the JB Ranch.

"Where do we go now, Cord?" Earl asked.

Cord raised an arm and pointed.

"Weatherall's ranch lies yonder. We'll make a wide circle and scout it from a distance."

"Do you expect to . . . ?"

"I expect to spill some blood before the sun sets," Cord said.

Earl smiled. "That's what I wanted to hear, Cord."

"You mind what I say to you, Earl. The dangerous part is not far away."

Earl nodded as Cord rode off in the direction of Horace's ranch.

The sun was just past noon and Cord knew that Weatherall's hands would be on full alert. They had started something by murdering Jesse and they knew that somebody would come looking for retribution.

Cord meant to see that the killers paid in full.

FIFTEEN

James Rowan rode in a wide circle beyond the corrals and nearby horse pastures. Horace had told him to make sure he could see anyone approaching from any direction.

Will Corwin was also on horseback, and he had a pair of binoculars up to his eyes. He was staked out on a line with the gully, watching to see if any of Barnes's hands came from that direction. He was very tense and nervous. Out of the corner of his eye, he could see Rowan, but it gave him little comfort.

The other hands were tending to the horses, but were also looking in all directions for any intruder.

Beyond the sight of Horace's men, Cord and Earl had stopped their horses in a low spot among small hillocks and ground-tied their horses.

"I don't see nothin'," Earl said.

"See those trees yonder?" Cord said.

"Just the tops of them."

"Well, they grow all the way to the ground and that's one of the concealments we'll use in our stalk. And most of what we do from now on is crawl."

"Crawl?"

"Yes, and I've got an important thing to tell you before we start."

Cord slid his rifle from its scabbard and nodded to Earl, who did the same.

"When you're stalking a man, Earl," Cord said, "the first thing you've got to think of is a way to back out from wherever you're going. It's not enough to come up on a man who may or may not be alone. You've got to figure that somebody is going to chase after you."

"That makes sense," Earl said.

"So, I put the horses here, where they're out of sight, and we'll take another course toward the ranch. Whoever we see will chase us from where we shot. They'll think we'll head back to our horses in a straight line."

"But we won't?"

"No. It will look like that until we cut back this way, behind all these little rolling hills. We'll be hunched over and close to the ground so they won't have a clear shot."

"Do you expect we'll find anyone beyond them trees?"

"Those are only some of the trees we'll use for cover. And yes, I expect Horace will have men on guard somewhere near the ranch house."

"You're pretty smart, Cord."

"We'll see how smart, little brother." Cord smiled and then hunched over. "Just follow my lead," he told Earl.

Earl crouched and followed his brother toward the tops of the trees in the distance.

They reached the first tree, an oak tree with a thick trunk.
There were two other small trees just beyond.

Cord hugged the tree and lowered himself. Earl followed
suit.

"See anything?" Earl whispered.

"Way off in the distance, I see someone on a horse. He's
not moving."

"Are we goin' after him?"

"Not yet," Cord said. "He can't be the only one out there.
He's holding something up to his head. I think it's a pair of
binoculars."

Cord strained to make out what the man on horseback
was doing. He saw the man turn his head and scan the trees.
Then the man slowly twisted his head and seemed to scan
the surrounding prairie.

Binoculars, no doubt about it.

That made it tricky for him and Earl, Cord thought.
Those lenses could pick up the least movement, the smallest
silhouette.

He hunkered down, deep in thought.

"What?" Earl whispered as he crouched down on his
haunches as well.

"Take off your hat, Earl. Put a rock on it so it won't blow
away."

Cord removed his hat and placed a stone on the brim.

"Cover your face with dirt," Cord said. "You may have
to spit on it for it to stick."

Earl watched as his brother scooped up a handful of dirt
and started rubbing it on his face. He did the same. And he
did have to spit on the dirt to make it cling to his face.

"Follow me and do whatever I do," Cord told his brother.
"It'll be slow going to get within range of that lookout."

"I know," Earl said.

Cord lay out flat and cradled his rifle. He began to crawl away from the trees, sliding on an angle that would bring him closer to the lookout.

As the two inched along, closing the gap between them and the man with the binoculars, a herd of pronghorn antelope appeared off to their left. The antelope grazed, but one was on sentry duty and as Cord froze, he saw that the lone antelope was staring in his direction.

"Uh-oh," he whispered.

Earl saw the antelope, then hugged the ground in imitation of his brother. They were a strange sight to him since he had never seen a pronghorn before.

They were graceful animals and their tawny and white coats glowed in the sunlight. He saw the sentry and wondered if the animal could see him.

Cord slowly raised his left hand and waggled it.

The lone antelope on guard snorted and wheeled, warning the rest of the small flock with his grunts and raised tail. The antelope galloped away and Cord breathed a sigh of relief.

He glanced toward the man with the binoculars and saw that he was gazing in the direction of the galloping antelope. But not anywhere near where Cord and his brother lay still.

Cord let out another breath of relief.

And the two crawled on, in an ever-shrinking arc.

Cord crawled to within two hundred yards of James Rowan, who was still peering through his binoculars, gazing in every direction.

Cord knew that the man was looking for riders on horseback. That was in Cord's favor. He could get closer. And as long as the man sat his horse, he would be a target at a closer range.

The two Wild brothers crawled ever closer.

When Cord figured they were within a hundred yards of the lookout, he stopped and slid his rifle from his cradling arms. He slipped it up and braced himself with his elbows. He placed the butt of his rifle against his shoulder and sighted down the barrel of the Winchester. He aligned the rear buckhorn to the blade front sight and leveled it on Rowan's chest.

Earl crawled up alongside and unlimbered his own rifle.

"Wait," Cord whispered.

He saw something else out of the corner of his eye.

Another rider.

The man appeared as a small speck on the horizon, but he rode toward the man with the binoculars. He, too, was looking all around, and he carried a rifle that rested on the pommel of his saddle.

Another lookout. A guard. Another one of Weatherall's hands, surely.

Cord turned his head slowly toward his brother.

"You sight on the man with the binoculars, Earl. I'll try and take down the other one when he comes closer."

"Okay," Earl whispered, and brought his rifle to bear on the first rider.

Earl took aim. But he had only the side of his target, so he had to steady his rifle. He wished it were Jessup in his sights. He did not know if Jessup was with Horace Weatherall, but he thought it was a strong possibility. And that was really the man he wanted to kill.

Cord leaned over close to Earl so that he could whisper into his ear.

"Remember," he said, "anyone watching will see our smoke and the flame from our muzzles. So after we shoot, we have to skedaddle."

Earl nodded. He lined up his sights again.

Cord leveled his barrel on the rider who had just arrived.

Cord had a frontal view, but the man's horse was tossing its head, blocking a clear shot to the chest.

Cord waited.

When the horse's head was down and his target's chest was exposed, he held his breath and squeezed the trigger.

A moment later, perhaps a half second later, Earl fired his rifle.

Cord saw the man he had shot throw up one arm and reel in the saddle. He thought he saw a puff of dust rise off the man's chest.

The first rider, James Rowan, spun around and dropped his binoculars as Earl's bullet ripped through his upper arm and entered his chest cavity. He gasped for a last breath as the main artery to his heart severed and his lungs filled with blood. The bullet ripped through his back and blood gushed through a fist-sized hole.

Rowan's rifle slid from the pommel and struck the ground, muzzle first. He clutched at the hole in his chest before he slumped over and fell sideways out of his saddle.

The man was dead before he hit the ground.

"Come on," Cord said to Earl as he slid backward, his rifle now at his side. He slid his hand up and grabbed it by the slightly warm barrel to keep the muzzle out of the dirt.

Neither he nor Earl reloaded, but both slid backward like lizards in reverse.

Then Cord rose to his feet and ran, hunched over, back to where they had left their hats.

Cord and Earl did not look back, but they heard distant shouts from what must have been the ranch house.

They ran fast and fell to their butts when they reached the trees. They quickly put on their hats. Then, still hunched over, they retreated to the place where they had tied their horses.

Both were out of breath when they climbed back into the saddle.

They sheathed their rifles and rode well away from the Weatherall ranch, toward the foothills and the mountains. They put spurs to their horses and galloped on to what Cord knew would be a safe haven.

"I got him, Cord," Earl said when they reached the safety of the foothills.

"I know," Cord said. "You shot well."

"You got your man, too. I saw him fall."

"That's only two," Cord said. "There are more. And some of them will be hunting us."

"I'm ready for them," Earl said.

Cord didn't say anything as they coursed through the low foothills and began to struggle up into the mountains. At one point, Cord stopped on a hill and looked down at the 2Bar2 Ranch. He saw men running around and saddling horses. They were tiny images, barely visible, but he knew he and his brother had put fear in those men down there.

Horace would know who had killed two of his men, Cord thought.

Now it was only a question of who would be next to die.

Cord pulled a stalk of rhubarb from his pocket and began to munch on it as they climbed ever higher up a mountain and entered heavy timber. Elk arose from their beds and moved away from them like wraiths in the shadowed solemnity of pines, spruce, fir, and juniper trees. Beams of sunlight glanced over the fallen pine needles and a hush rose up around them as they traversed a long stretch of flat ground beneath a massive outcropping of limestone rocks.

Now Cord would wait for nightfall and strike again under the cover of darkness.

SIXTEEN

The men on the 2Bar2 heard the shots like distant cracks of a bullwhip. They all turned their heads in the direction of their lookout, James. They heard two shots, close together, and wondered what they meant.

Horace looked at Harley Davis, who was pumping well water into a trough in one of the corrals.

"Finish up there so you can check on who fired those rifle shots," Horace told him.

"Finishin' up," Davis said and stopped pumping water into the trough. His horse was close by. He mounted up and rode off in the direction he knew James Rowan had been posted.

He returned twenty minutes later, his face drawn and pale.

"James is dead," he told Horace. "So is Will Corwin. One bullet hole in each man."

"Any sign of the shooter?"

"Nope. He got clean away. Nary a sign of any shooter."

"It was that damned Wild," Horace said. "Gather up all the men, Harley. I want to talk to all hands."

"Yes, sir," he said and rode off to gather up all the hands on Weatherall's ranch.

Horace sent men out to retrieve the dead lookouts and their horses and bring them back for burial. When they returned, he looked at the bodies and felt his anger rise in him.

He told the small assemblage of men what he wanted.

"I'm upping the reward money for anyone who kills Wild," he said. "Two hundred dollars. Harley," he said to Davis, "I want you to bring in our man on the JB Ranch. You know who I mean. He's no longer needed there, but I need him."

Davis nodded and separated from the other men. "I'll go get him," he said to Horace.

"The rest of you may notice that our numbers have thinned. I expect more men soon, and more horses, when my brother, Abner, gets here from Missouri. In the meantime, I want you to put most of our stock out to pasture and hunt down Cord Wild. That's my main priority. Be careful and hunt hard. I want his scalp and his hide."

The men dispersed as Harley rode off toward the JB Ranch.

Horace left for town a half hour later with cash from his safe. He wanted to see the banker who held the mortgage on the JB Ranch, one Jeremy Conway, at the Cheyenne Bank & Trust. He wanted that ranch and he meant to buy up the mortgage and foreclose on Jesse's widow.

Ernesto noticed that Danny Larrimore had been more secretive since the death of their boss, Jesse Barnes. Ernesto had had suspicions about Danny for some time, but when he saw him ride out, away from the ranch house and corrals, he followed at a distance.

Danny rode to a grove of oak trees out of sight of the house and stayed for some time. Then he rode back to the ranch, taking a different route.

Ernesto went into the grove and looked at all the trees. Two of them grew close together and he saw a note in the crotch where the two trees joined. He retrieved it and read it.

Widow broke. Needs another loan. Daughter offering to go to work. No sign of Wild.

Ernesto put the note back.

A rage built up in him. Danny had betrayed them. He thought about the ride with him when they'd tracked the stolen mares.

Danny had known where to go. Yes, he glanced at the tracks, but he knew all along that he was leading Jesse into a trap. It was the same when they reached the gully. Danny had seen the tracks leading away, but had not seemed surprised.

He wished Wild were here. Danny was a dangerous man. Nobody knew much about him, but he was from somewhere in Missouri.

He must have known Horace Weatherall and gone to work for Jesse just to spy on him.

The thought that Danny was a traitor to the brand made Ernesto sick to his stomach. He felt as if he would puke just thinking about such a betrayal.

And he didn't know what to do about it. He could tell Abigail, but then she would be even more devastated. He could confront Danny and call him out, but that would be perilous. Danny was fast on the draw and he was a dead shot.

If only Cord Wild were here, Ernesto could go to him. Cord would know what to do, and if Cord confronted Danny, then Danny was a dead man.

Ernesto decided to keep silent about Danny for now. None of the other men would dare go against the quick-drawing traitor, so Ernesto would just wait until he could talk to Wild. That was the safest thing to do, and the smartest.

He would just keep an eye on Danny for any suspicious activity. That was what he could do until Wild returned.

He hoped it would be enough to keep Abigail and Lelia from any harm.

But when Ernesto tried to find Danny late that afternoon, there was no sign of him anywhere on the ranch.

He went to the bunkhouse and saw that Danny's foot-locker was unlocked. He opened it and saw that it was empty. He asked the other men if they had seen Danny and they all replied in the negative.

Danny was no longer on the JB Ranch.

He was gone, and Ernesto walked around in a daze and with a heavy heart for the rest of the day. He had a secret and he could tell no one but Cord Wild.

SEVENTEEN

Horace rode back to the ranch just before nightfall. He had persuaded the banker to sell him the JB mortgage, which would be in arrears in less than a month.

Danny Larrimore was waiting for him, and the two entered the house. As Horace closed the door, he called out to one of his men.

"Bring Jessup to the house," he said.

"What's up?" Danny asked.

"Any sign of Wild at the JB?" Horace asked. He waved Danny to a hard-backed chair and sat down in one covered in buffalo hide with a baronial backrest and large stuffed arms.

The front room was stocked with rifles and pistols hanging on pegs, and a couple of Currier & Ives prints of New York streets hung on the wall in wooden frames. He also had a large painting of a racehorse with four white stockings and a blaze face.

"Didn't see him." Danny took off his hat and looked at Horace with pale blue eyes that looked vacant and cold.

"Too bad," Horace said. "He killed two of my men today."

"The hell you say."

"Shot 'em down like dogs. Neither man had a chance."

"That don't sound like Wild. He usually works in close and gives a man a chance."

"Not this time. He was some distance when he fired. May have had somebody else shoot the other one. The fellers who went out there found where they both lay down and fired their rifles."

"The hell you say," Danny said again.

"So I called you back in for a tracking job."

"Wild?"

"Yes. I want you to hunt that bastard down and kill him. And I'm offering you a generous reward if you bring me back his head. But keep the amount of the reward to yourself."

"Will do," Danny said. "How much of a reward?"

"Five hundred dollars."

Danny whistled. "That's more money than I've seen in a long while."

"My way is clear to take over the JB Ranch. I bought up the paper today at the bank. Just a matter of time before the land is in my hands."

"You still got money left from that Missouri bank job?"

"Yeah, I do. I'm a saver and I'm frugal," Horace said.

"You are, I know."

There was a knock on the door.

"Come in," Horace called.

Bart Jessup opened the door and walked into the front room. "You called for me?" he said to Horace. Then he saw Danny, who rose from his chair.

"Bart, what in hell are you doin' here?" Danny asked. "I thought you was with Abner."

"I was," Jessup said. "He's on his way, with thirty head of horses."

The two men embraced briefly.

"Have a seat, Jessup," Horace said.

"That true? Your brother is a-comin' here?" Danny asked.

"So Jessup said. He can tell you all about it later. I wanted you to know he was here and that Abner will bring more men with him."

"Sounds like you got it all figured out, Horace," Danny said.

"Most of it. It all depends on you right now."

"Just point me where Wild was and I'll get to trackin'," Danny said.

"Bart," Horace said, "you saw where Wild and the other man lit out when they killed my men this morning."

"Yeah. We found signs in a clump of trees, then some trampled grass. That led us to where they tied their horses. They were pretty slick."

"Take Danny out there and show him. Maybe he can track Wild down before he does any more damage."

"Sure. We got plenty of daylight left," Jessup said.

"Fine. Danny, I'm counting on you."

Horace rose from his chair, dismissing the two men. They both left and he walked to the window and watched them as they talked over old times.

Danny and Jessup had grown up together back in Missouri. Both had been with Horace when he started robbing banks. Later, Jessup had gone to work with Abner, while Horace had brought Danny to Wyoming. Both were good hunters, but Danny was the better tracker.

Now, all he had to do was wait for his brother to arrive with the horses stolen from the Wild ranch, and for Danny to kill Cordwainer Wild.

He rubbed his hands in anticipation of the wealth that would one day be his.

And his alone.

EIGHTEEN

Cord reined up as they left the timber. They had to cross a bare, almost grassless stretch of ground. He dismounted, handed his reins to Earl, and walked back to a large spruce tree.

"What are you doing?" Earl asked.

"Cutting us some brooms," Cord said.

As Earl watched, Cord crawled under the tree and drew his knife. He cut off two long-needled branches and returned to his horse. He handed one of the branches to Earl.

"Follow me in single file," he said, "and drag that branch behind you. Switch it back and forth like I do."

They rode across the open spot, brushing away their tracks behind them. When they reached the timber on the other side, Cord halted and looked back.

"Good job," he said.

"No tracks that I can see."

"You never know who might be on your trail up here," Cord said.

They saw more elk in the next stand of timber. The cows arose from their beds, and their young ones traipsed after them as they slunk away over deadfalls and around brush until they were all gone.

The Wild brothers climbed higher, past large rocky outcroppings, and Cord stopped over one of these where the ground was flat.

"We'll stay here," he said as he dismounted and tied Windmill to a grassy spot where a small juniper grew.

Earl dismounted and found a spot for his horse. Cord heard him talk to the animal and call the gelding "Louie."

"That the name you gave that horse, Earl?" Cord asked.

"Yeah. That's his name."

"Didn't you have a puppy named that when you were just a tyke?"

"Yeah, I did. Louie died, so I gave the name to my horse."

They sat and leaned against two pine trees. Cord chewed on a stalk of rhubarb while Earl gnawed on hardtack.

"Do you think they'll come after us?" Earl asked.

"Likely, they'll look for us. I don't think any of Horace's men are good trackers. Not here in the mountains."

"Good. I'd hate to be surprised by any of 'em ridin' up on us."

"We'll go back down early in the morning," Cord said.

"Not tonight?"

"Let 'em sleep. Before dawn, those who are up for early chores will be drowsy and the rest will be asleep. He has only a few men left, I reckon."

"That sounds okay to me."

They were silent for several moments. Then Cord finished his rhubarb and wiped his hands together.

"How do you feel about killing a man, Earl?" Cord asked.

Earl thought about that for several moments before he answered. "When I shot that man, I wasn't thinking he was human," Earl said. "I didn't have no feelings at all until I saw him fall off his horse."

"And then what?"

"It was kind of like killin' a chicken. Or a coon. I felt, well, kind of good that I had done it."

"Didn't you think about the man? That you cut his life short?"

"Not right then I didn't. Later, I felt kind of sick inside. Why? What do you feel when you kill a man?"

"It's a heavy weight on a man's shoulders, to take a human life," Cord said.

"So, you feel bad afterward?"

"I don't think of just that one man, but of the whole human race," Cord said.

"You do?"

"When you take a life, you are subtracting something from the earth, from the entire universe. Then I wonder about all the people who are alive, who were born just like us and raised and taught to obey the government and its laws. And I wonder why some men break those laws and are caught and hanged or shot in front of a firing squad. And I begin to think about men and civilization itself. I wonder why people are born and then they die, either of old age, of disease, or at the hands of another."

"Holy cow, that's a lot to think about," Earl said.

"It is. But that's what I think about. And I think about the preacher who talks about heaven and another life after this one."

"Do you believe that stuff, Cord?"

"I think about it. Everything on earth dies. We are here for a very short time. I wonder why."

"Why do you think?"

"It doesn't make much sense to me that we are born and given life, and then die. What is our purpose in being here in the first place? Or is there something beyond this one? Is there such a place as heaven or the Happy Hunting Grounds? If so, what do we do there? What would be the purpose of that kind of life?"

"Boy, you really think deep, don't you?" Earl said.

"I wonder what happens with all of men's accomplishments after they die. What happens to the minds of men who wrote books or composed beautiful music or painted pictures? What happens to the music? Does it go to heaven where others can enjoy it, or does it just stay here?"

"I never thought about any of that stuff," Earl said.

"Well, I do. All the time. Especially when I have to kill a man and cut his life short."

"Do you feel guilty?"

"We picked those men off like squirrels," Cord said. "I feel bad about just shooting them down like that."

"How come?"

"They didn't have the chance to defend themselves. They were not allowed to spend those last few moments of life thinking about why they were going to die. They had no chance to think about eternity."

"So you'd give them a chance to kill us?"

"I'd want the edge, Earl. But to shoot a man down from a distance is wrong. It makes me sick that I did that today."

"Come to think of it, it makes me a little sick, too."

"It won't happen again."

"No. Those men are killers. They murdered your friend."

"I know. But a man has to live with himself. I killed that man the same way he, or his friends, killed Jesse Barnes. But was killing that way justified? I don't think so."

"You're too hard on yourself, Cord."

Cord spit out a chunk of fibrous stalk that he couldn't chew.

"Well, I won't make that mistake again," he said. "That shot makes me no better than the man I killed or the man who hired him."

"So what are you going to do next time?"

Cord looked up at the sky. He breathed a deep breath.

"We are given life. Maybe for a purpose, Earl. It's up to us to make it what it is. If we don't have a code to follow, we are just sheep. We follow. We eat. We die. We leave no footprints."

"So?"

"So, it's what a man does that makes him human, that makes him a man. I don't want to go through life as a heartless killer."

"But you want justice. You believe in justice. You believe a man must pay for his crimes."

"Sure. But who sets me up as judge and jury? Who gives me the right to be God?"

"Where there is no law . . . ," Earl said.

"You're right, Earl. In a way. Where there is no law, one man, or many men, must become the law. There is such a thing as justice. And I believe in it. But justice is blind, and I wonder if I am supposed to be its eyes."

Their talk ended there and they waited for sunset.

No man tracked them that day.

They slept, and some hours before dawn, Cord woke up and shook his brother awake.

"It's time," he said. "Time to face the enemy."

They rode down to the 2Bar2 Ranch and, on foot,

prowled around the bunkhouse. They listened to the snores of men inside and the soft nickers of horses in the corrals.

They waited for a lamp to be lighted and for the first man to heed the call of nature and leave the bunkhouse.

They waited, their hands on their pistol grips in the chill before dawn.

NINETEEN

Lamplight illuminated the window of the bunkhouse. Cord crouched between that window and the front door. He heard a rustling from inside and the gravelly voice of a man who had suddenly awakened.

Springs creaked as the men inside stirred. Cord heard footsteps and the clang of a coffeepot. Soft voices announced that they were awake. He tried to count the number of different voices and could only discern four or five.

Finally, one man emerged from the bunkhouse. It appeared that he was going to head for the nearby outhouse. When he was clear of the steps and on firm ground, the man stiffened as he felt something hard and cold in his side.

Cord shoved the barrel of his pistol into the soft flesh of the man's side. He cocked the hammer back. The click was loud in the silence of the predawn.

"Not a sound," Cord said.

The man nodded.

"This way," Cord whispered and pointed toward the out-house. When they were a few feet away from the outhouse, Cord stopped and faced the man.

"What's your name?" he asked.

"Orson Farrell," the man said.

"Do you know who I am?" Cord asked.

"You're the one they call the Wild Gun, ain't you?"

"Close enough. Do you know how close you are to death, Mr. Farrell?"

"Pretty close, I reckon."

Earl watched from the other side of the bunkhouse door, fascinated.

"Good guess. I'm going to give you a choice, Mr. Farrell."

"What's that?"

"You can saddle up and ride away from this ranch and we'll call it quits. You'll live. But if you stay here or ever come back, I'll kill you. What's your choice?"

"I'll saddle up," Farrell said.

"Make it quick," Cord told him. He stepped away and watched as Farrell walked toward the stables. He was unarmed and still in his nightshirt.

Cord walked back to stand next to the door.

He looked at Earl.

Moments later, they heard hoofbeats and saw a shadowy figure on horseback. Farrell rode away at a rapid gallop.

That's when another man emerged from the bunkhouse. He yawned and stretched his arms upward as he clumped down the steps.

He stopped when he felt the cold steel of Cord's pistol punch him in the layer of fat ringing his side.

"What the hell?"

"Not a word if you want to live," Cord said.

"Damn you," the man said without thinking.

"Step out," Cord said. "And keep your mouth shut."

The man nodded, his hands up in the air.

A few feet away, Cord moved the pistol and stuck the barrel square in the man's belly.

"Do you know who I am?" he asked.

"You the Wild Gun?"

"I am, and your time on this ranch is up."

"What do you mean?"

"I mean you're not going to work here anymore. You're not going to shoot down any more innocent men."

"I didn't . . ."

"Don't lie. What's your name?"

"Colby. Ted Colby."

"Well, Ted, you've got a choice to make."

"Huh? What choice?"

"The same as I gave your friend Farrell. You can saddle up and head for Cheyenne and then parts farther out, or you can die right where you stand. It just takes a little squeeze of this trigger and your guts will churn to mush."

"Jesus," Colby said.

"Your choice, Colby. Live or die."

"I reckon I'll ride out. Hell, that ain't no choice."

"It's the only one I'm giving you," Cord said.

"I'm gone, then," Colby said.

Cord shoved him toward the stables and watched the man stumble to where his horse was boarded for the night.

"Cord, look out," Earl called from the doorway as Colby reached in his back pocket and pulled out a small pistol.

Cord crouched as Colby whirled around and cocked the .32 revolver.

Colby pointed his pistol straight at Cord.

Cord leveled his pistol and squeezed the trigger. The

explosion was loud in the predawn quiet. Flame and smoke spurted from the muzzle of his pistol.

His bullet slammed into Colby's chest just as Colby squeezed the trigger of his pistol. His bullet plowed a furrow in front of Cord and died in the dirt before it reached his boots.

Colby tumbled forward as blood spurted from the hole in his chest. He gurgled as more blood rose in his throat. He gasped and kicked after he hit the ground. His hand relaxed as the .32 Smith & Wesson slid from his lifeless grasp.

He gave a last scratchy sigh and died.

Cord spun around as yells erupted from inside the bunkhouse.

"What in hell was that?" someone shouted from inside.

"Earl, get to your horse," Cord yelled and started running toward Windmill.

The two reached their horses and climbed into their saddles as the bunkhouse door flew open and men with pistols and rifles in their hands jammed the doorway. They turned their heads right and left as Cord and Earl rode off into the darkness.

A lamp came on in Horace's house in the upstairs bedroom.

Three men poured through the doorway of the bunkhouse and swung their weapons, each looking for a target.

"Who the hell shot?" Jessup asked. He swung his pistol in a wide arc.

"Look, over there," called another.

The men rushed to where Colby lay.

"It's Ted Colby," Jessup said. "Dead."

"Shit," said another man as he crouched and looked all around him.

"It's that Wild feller," Nestor Jones growled.

"Where's Farrell?" one man asked. "He come out here?"

"Orson," called out another, cupping a hand to his mouth. No answer.

"I heard a horse ride away a while ago," Jones said. "Or at least I thought I heard one at a gallop."

"Orson must have lit a shuck before Colby come out."

"This is a hell of a note," Jessup said.

"Nobody's safe here," Nestor said. "I'm gettin' the hell out."

"He'll hunt you down. They don't call him 'the Wild Gun' for nothin'."

"You don't know nothin'," Nestor said to Pete Gander. "You ain't never seen that jasper."

"No, I ain't, but I seen what he done," Pete said.

The men had started to walk back to the bunkhouse when Horace emerged out of the darkness.

"What's goin' on here?" he asked.

"I told Ted that peashooter he carries would get him in trouble," Pete said.

"What in hell are you talkin' about?" Horace demanded.

"Colby's dead," Jessup said. "And Farrell is missing."

"What?" Horace exclaimed.

"Over yonder," Pat said as he pointed to Colby's body.

Horace walked over and looked at the dead man.

"He's dead, all right. Anybody see anything? Who shot him?"

The men shrugged and shook their heads.

"You lily-livered baboons. Wild came here right under your damned noses and shot Ted. No tellin' what he did to Farrell."

"We heard galloping hoofbeats a while ago," Pete said. "Farrell must have lit out."

"Damn," Horace said.

He looked at the remainder of his men and wagged a finger at them.

"You're a worthless bunch," he said. "A man walks up here and does what he wants to do while you bunch of blind bastards let him do it. Well, if you don't watch out, you'll be next. That Wild Gun is one loco bastard, but he's a dead shot."

The men's heads drooped as Horace raged at them, cursing them, calling them every name that came to his tongue.

Horace walked back to his house. He was still angry. Wild threatened to ruin everything, all his plans, his dreams, his hopes.

Where in hell was his tracker, Danny? He wondered. Had Wild killed him, too? There was no one else he could trust to track down and kill Wild. And somehow, Wild had eluded Danny.

But maybe, he thought, Danny was still alive and would come through for Horace.

And if not, well, Wild would eventually come for him.

The thought made Horace even angrier. But his hands turned clammy and sweat soaked his forehead as he sat down in his chair and aimed his pistol at the front door.

Just in case.

TWENTY

Danny had tracked Cord and Earl until it got too dark for him to see.

But he knew the direction they had headed after entering the mountains. He would wait until morning and then pick up their trail in daylight.

He began to track his quarry at first light. There were plenty of signs, with hoofprints in the vacant spots between layers of pine needles. He looked for disturbed or broken branches on saplings and brush. He also looked for scrapes in the pine needles where one or both horses dragged their hooves.

It was not the easiest trail to follow, but Danny had learned to track wild game at an early age. He was fascinated by the tracks of quail and squirrel, wild turkey, rabbits, and bobcats in the Ozark wilderness of Missouri.

He came to the bare ground where Cord and Earl had swept away their tracks. He could see that the ground had been disturbed, but as he crossed that place, he had to look long and hard for any signs that they had entered the timber.

But there *were* signs.

There were scuffed patches in the pine needles, a crushed branch on a juniper bush. Slowly, he made his way through the timber and realized that the tracks led in a more or less straight line. And he found the cut spruce branches that the pair of men had discarded.

Then he came to the place where Cord and Earl had spent most of the night. There were depressions where they had sat and others where they had lain out flat.

He made a circle to find the tracks leading from that spot. He found signs that they had descended from the mountain and entered into the foothills.

Now he knew where they were headed.

He was still in the timber, heading downslope toward the foothills, when Danny drew up short.

A sound.

His heartbeat quickened.

There was something out there. Heading his way.

He backed his horse farther into the timber and walked him sideways until his body was behind a pine tree and a spruce.

Somebody was surely riding up and they were in a hurry.

Heavy footfalls. Crashing through brush.

The breathy wheeze of a horse.

The creak of leather. Men in the saddles. At least two horses, he figured.

Danny waited, listening intently. He separated sounds, judged the terrain, heard a rock dislodge and roll downhill a short distance.

All these things put pictures in Danny's mind. Years of tracking had made his senses acute. He knew what was coming up into the timber.

And he had a pretty good idea who it was.

He peered from behind the tree as the sounds grew closer. He leaned from the saddle so that just his head cleared the pine tree. Closer and closer came the sounds of two horses. They were climbing, clawing with their hooves for a foothold in grass and rocks, brushing against second-growth saplings.

At first, he saw nothing but trees and brush. Then, some distance away, he caught a glimpse of a shirt, a man's arm. Then these disappeared and he saw the shoulders of a smaller man. Just for a second or two.

His pulse sped up as the thrill of discovery coursed in his veins, his sinews.

Then the sounds stopped.

Danny drew his head back behind the tree. He listened.

The riders had stopped.

Why?

He had made no sound. His horse was quiet. The animal stood still, its ears pricked. He listened to the sound of his own breathing. Slow and steady. He listened to his horse's breath through its nostrils. He listened for sounds where he had last seen parts of two men.

Dead silence. Cord reined up, put a finger to his lips as he turned around to look at Earl.

Earl reined up and his brow wrinkled as he wondered why his brother had stopped.

The horses were not too winded. He felt his horse's ribs as they flexed.

Cord had heard something. Or something was not right.

Earl sat his saddle in silence. He studied his brother.

Cord's head twisted and he cupped a hand to one ear. Then he sat very still and raised an arm.

Cord pointed to his right, toward an outcropping of limestone just inside the timber.

Earl nodded. He knew his brother wanted him to follow him to a safer place, away from the direction they had been heading.

Then Cord touched spurs gently to Windmill's flanks. He tugged on the reins so that the horse only took a single step to its right. He slowly walked Windmill over to the rocky outcropping, then dismounted. He climbed atop the rock bluff and beckoned to Earl to dismount and climb up there with him.

"What's the matter, Cord?" Earl whispered once he sat down next to his brother.

"I don't know."

"Did you hear something? See something?"

"I felt something," Cord whispered.

"What?"

"A feeling that someone was watching us. You know how it is. You feel eyes on the back of your neck and you turn around and someone is staring at you."

Earl nodded. He knew the feeling.

Still, they seemed alone, surrounded only by trees. Even the elk were not moving, nor the mule deer. It was quiet.

Cord picked up a small stone.

He threw it off the rock and into the timber. The rock made a sound and rolled a foot or two.

Cord put two fingers to his lips in a demand for Earl to keep quiet.

Danny heard the sound of the rock and wondered what it was. He strained his ears to listen for any other sound. All he knew was that the two horsemen had disappeared. He hadn't heard them, so he knew they had sneaked out of earshot.

Where were they?

He slowly dismounted. The stirrup took his weight and creaked. He stood there for a long moment. He listened for any sound.

But there was no sound.

He took slow steps to where he had seen the horsemen. He examined the ground and saw the hoofmarks, the disturbed earth and pine needles. He looked into the timber and saw the bare outline of the limestone bluff, a large outcropping of solid rock.

And that was the direction the tracks were leading.

He sucked in a breath and gripped the butt of his pistol. Then he started following the horse tracks.

U p on the bluff, Cord saw a bush move. He heard the soft sound of a foot crushing the ground. Then he saw a denimed leg take another step.

He drew his pistol. There was the slithering sound of metal brushing against leather.

The approaching man stopped.

"That's far enough," Cord called out.

He saw the leg stiffen and then saw a man's shirt, and a second later, his face came into view.

Cord recognized the man. He knew only that he worked for Jesse Barnes as a horse wrangler.

"Danny, that you?" Cord said.

"Yep. Can't see you, Cord. Show yourself."

"Step into the open, Danny."

Danny took a step or two until he came into full view of Cord atop the rocky ledge.

"That's far enough, Danny," Cord said. "You tracking me?"

Danny didn't answer right away. He peered in the direction of Cord's voice. But he still couldn't see him.

"Just huntin', Cord," Danny said.

"In a pig's eye," Cord responded.

"Elk," Danny said. "Meat for the ranch."

"Like hell. You're following horse tracks."

Danny's right hand flexed on the butt of his pistol.

"You jerk that Colt and you're a dead man, Danny," Cord said.

"Habit," Danny said and raised his hand from the pistol grip.

He thought about the five-hundred-dollar bounty on Cord's head. The man was so close, although Danny could not see him. Easy money if he could get a shot.

"No need to worry, Wild. I ain't huntin' you. Let's chew the fat some. Come down and we'll talk."

"Like hell, Danny. You don't hunt for Jesse nor anybody else. You just stay right where you are."

Danny saw the barest of movements atop the bluff. He said nothing. But his right arm bent at the elbow as his hand descended toward the butt of his pistol. He spread his feet a little wider apart.

Cord saw the movements. He cocked his pistol.

In the silence, the sound was very loud, like a metal door opening on a blazing furnace. Like a door opening into hell.

"You even twitch, Danny, and you'll never draw another breath."

"Go to hell," Danny said and stepped to one side, toward a pine tree. He drew his pistol in one quick snatch.

Cord took dead aim on Danny as he moved. He saw the flash of metal from the barrel of Danny's pistol as a shaft of sunlight beamed down on it.

An eternity seemed to pass before Cord squeezed the trigger.

At the same time, Danny's pistol rose up and the man squeezed the trigger of his Colt.

Explosions ripped through the silence.

Bullets whizzed through the air like angry hornets.

Death was a pair of lead projectiles speeding toward living flesh and bone.

TWENTY-ONE

Abner Weatherall skirted Cheyenne. He and his two men drove the horses at a fast walk over the prairie toward the 2Bar2. He wore a smile of satisfaction as he saw the smoke rising from chimneys and the roofs of buildings in the distance.

He knew he did not have far to go and he was anxious to see Horace.

"When I give the signal, run 'em on to the ranch at a gallop," he called back to the other two men on the flanks of the herd.

They both nodded and grinned.

When he saw the boundary to Horace's ranch, he raised his hand and spurred his own horse. The horses picked up speed and started running. They streamed onto Weatherall land and headed for the corrals and the barn and stables.

The two hands yelled and whooped as they chased the horses.

Abner halted and wheeled his horse to stop the driven horses. He waved his hat and the horses turned and came to a halt in puffs of dust.

Horace came out of the barn with a smile on his face. The few men left to him stopped what they were doing to admire the horses Abner had brought all the way from Missouri.

"Ho, Abner," Horace called. "Been lookin' for you."

"Howdy, brother Horace. We're here after driving these horses clear across Kansas."

"We'll put 'em up," Horace said and started barking orders to his men.

"Light down and come on into the house."

Abner looked long and hard at one of the men rounding up all the loose horses.

"Hello, Bart," he called to Jessup. "We wondered where you was at."

"Long story," Jessup said.

"Can't wait to hear it," Abner said as he swung out of the saddle.

He followed Horace into the ranch house, a place he had visited before, but not in a long while. He took off his hat and beat its brim against his leg as he walked into the front room. Dust rose from his denims as Horace waved him to a chair.

"Well, you got here," Horace said. "Pretty good time, too."

"We made a good fifteen miles a day, sometimes twenty if we drove 'em long enough into the night."

"Any trouble?"

"Nope. We run into some buffalo in west Kansas, but they up and ran when I whooped at 'em. Saw a lot of antelope and we shot a couple, cooked 'em. Tasted like bad pork."

Horace laughed.

"We had to kill old man Wild. His kid come and chased after Jessup. Glad to see he's still alive. When we was ridin' away, we saw smoke. I don't know what happened, but somebody must've started a fire."

"That's interesting," Horace said. "Jessup didn't say nothin' about no fire."

"Barn or house, I reckon. Just somethin' we saw when we looked back. Lots of smoke in the sky."

"Well, you're here. That's all that matters, and we might take over some more land and really build us a herd of good horseflesh."

"That sounds good to me. I come to stay, Horace."

"Good. Want a drink? I got some good whiskey in that cupboard over yonder."

"I could use a taste. Wash out the trail dust."

Abner crossed his legs and watched his brother go over to a cabinet. Horace brought out a bottle and two glasses, poured whiskey in both of them.

They clinked glasses together and drank, then both sat back down.

"So, what's this about expanding your ranch, Horace?" Abner asked.

Horace told him about the killing of Jesse Barnes and his buying the mortgage for the ranch.

"So, there's only Barnes's widow and a daughter, and I'm pretty sure they can't make the mortgage payment next month. Not unless they sell some of their horses between now and then."

"So it's not a sure thing," Abner said.

"What do you mean?"

"If they make their payments, they keep the ranch, Horace. Plain and simple."

"Well, yeah. But I'm pretty sure they won't. I'll kick them off the ranch and take over the land and all the stock."

"What if Barnes didn't leave any heirs?" Abner said.

"But he did."

"What if he didn't?"

"Then the loan would be in default and I'd have what I want."

"That's just it," Abner said. "You have to get rid of the heirs."

"Meaning?"

"Meaning, you eliminate them two women."

Horace sipped his drink and sat back in his chair, deep in thought. Then he let out a breath of air through pursed lips.

"I don't know," he said. "You mean kill them two women?"

"Yep. That's exactly what I mean. That's how you get rid of the competition."

"That's a tall order, Abner."

"I got a man who can do the job. You know him. He was with us when we robbed that bank in West Plains."

"Who?"

"Eddie Lomax. He come with me when we stole the horses. He likes to hurt women. His blood runs ice cold when it comes to that."

"Oh, I remember. When we knocked over that bank, he bloodied one of the women there when he pistol-whipped her."

"And he beat up on Lucas Wild's old lady when we took them horses."

"Hmmm," breathed Horace.

"We all raped that Wild woman, but Eddie beat her up pretty bad while he was jumpin' on her."

"Yeah, yeah. So you think he might . . ."

"Eddie will do what I tell him to, Horace. He'll kill those women, and you've got yourself another ranch."

"I don't know. It's a mighty big step."

"I could run it for you. I ain't goin' back to Missouri. And we've got thirty more horses. That's cash on the hoof, Horace."

"You make a good argument. Getting rid of those two women would sure speed things up. And I would need more hands with that other ranch. Wild has killed some of my men, drove off another. And you could stay over at the Barncs spread and do our breeding and such."

Abner grinned. He drank from his glass and wiped his lips.

"You're getting the picture, Horace. We'll be partners, but each have our own spread."

Horace finished his drink and smacked his lips.

"Let's talk to Eddie Lomax," Horace said. "He's got to do it without making much noise."

"Eddie's an expert at these things. He'll have his way with the women and then choke 'em both to death."

"And leave no tracks, no trail to us?"

"He'll go in at night and nobody will know the difference," Abner said.

"Let's do it," Horace said.

The two got up from their chairs and embraced.

Then they walked outside to find Eddie Lomax.

Horace felt good for the first time in days. He saw his dream coming true even sooner than he realized.

He felt a surge of power in every fiber of his being.

And if Danny killed Wild, all would be well in his world.

TWENTY-TWO

Danny's bullet was slightly wide of the mark. It spanged into the rock next to Cord and caromed harmlessly into the timber. Cord's face stung with shattered fragments of limestone.

Danny felt a burning sensation as Cord's bullet burned a furrow in the upper part of his leg. It ripped through his denim trousers like a firebrand. He fell against the pine tree and realized his bullet had missed its target.

Cord lifted his pistol to take aim for another shot.

Danny circled the tree until it was between him and Cord.

Cord held his fire while Danny breathed hard behind his shield.

He beckoned to Earl, who crabbed over close to him.

"Earl, you hug this rock while I try to get at that gunny."

Earl nodded as Cord crawled off the rock and soundlessly

walked in a semicircle to a place where he could see Danny behind the tree.

It took him several moments, but then he saw the man, who was looking backward as he leaned against the pine tree.

Danny's pistol was in his right hand. Cord waited until he turned around and the pistol was visible. Danny held it pointed straight down by his knee. He was waiting to lift it and take another shot.

Cord took aim on Danny's hand. The hand that held the pistol.

He drew in a breath, held it; as he started to exhale, he squeezed the trigger.

Danny yowled as the bullet smashed through the slender bones of his hand. The pistol dropped like a chunk of useless metal from his hand. Blood spurted from the shattered hand and Danny hopped on one foot, away from the tree. He screamed in pain and looked straight at Cord.

Cord stood there, a few feet away, a tendril of smoke rising from the barrel of his pistol. He recocked his Colt and blew away the shawl of white smoke that drifted like a cobweb over his face.

"Your shootin' days are over, Danny," Cord said.

Danny bent over to retrieve his pistol with his gun hand. But his fingers did not work and blood dripped from his hand like a leaking faucet.

"Damn you, Wild," Danny spat.

"Come on down, Earl," Cord called to the top of the rock. He heard a scrambling noise and knew his brother had heard him.

Moments later, Earl stood by his side, pistol in hand.

"Are you going to finish him, Cord?" he asked.

"No, I'm going to let Danny live."

"Why?"

"I'm going to make a messenger out of him."

"Go to hell," Danny said as he gripped his wrist. His hand still bled and dripped on the ground, spattering against the metal of his pistol.

He drew himself up straight and stared at the pistol in Cord's hand.

"You're the one who's going there, Danny," Cord said. "But first you're going to take a message back to Horace."

"Message? What message?"

"I could kill you now, Danny, but I'm going to let you live. I want you to tell Horace that I'm coming for him. He won't know when, but he's going to die."

"You'll never get to Horace, you fool," Danny said. "He'll have your head on his mantel before you even get close."

"Just give him the message, Danny. That his days are short and numbered."

"What if I don't? What are you going to do about it?"

"We're going to ride you down to the 2Bar2 where he can see you. Earl and I will be your escort."

"Damn you, Wild." Danny pulled his hand up until it was level. He looked at Cord and his eyes fisted shut as the pain shot up his arm. The hand was useless and the pad on his palm had been shot away. It was just a mass of torn flesh. Several crucial bones were splintered and their sharp ends stuck out through what was left of the flesh on the top part of his hand. Tears leaked from his squeezed eyes.

"Damn, damn, damn," Danny wailed.

"Earl, go find his horse and bring it here," he told his brother. "And holster your pistol. You won't be needing it anytime soon."

Earl shoved his pistol back in his holster and walked away, downslope, to look for Danny's horse.

Cord stepped up close to Danny and shoved him away from the tree. Then he stooped over and picked up the man's bloody pistol.

Danny looked on with scorn and pain.

"I paid good money for that Colt," Danny said.

"I expect you did. But you won't be needing this firearm anymore, Danny. Your bushwhacking days are over."

"I still got one more hand."

"You keep that up, and I'll smash that one to a pulp, too."

"Wild, you're a pure bastard. Know that? Just a damned bastard."

"I 'spect you know all about bastards, Danny, you being one of 'em."

Danny scowled as more pain shot through the muscles and nerves of his wrist and arm. Bloud spouted from the wound.

Cord shoved Danny's pistol inside his belt after he wiped the barrel on his trousers.

Earl trudged up the slope. He led Danny's horse.

"Take that rifle out of its boot," Cord told his brother. "You can secure it to your own saddle after we help Danny mount up."

Cord grabbed Danny by the elbow of his good arm and shoved him toward his horse as Earl slipped the rifle from its scabbard.

"I ain't gettin' on my horse," Danny said, and he shoved backward with his good arm.

"You're going to ride, if I have to tie you to your horse, Danny."

Cord shoved him toward the horse.

"I can't pull myself up with this game hand," Danny said.

"We'll lift you up," Cord said.

Earl laid the rifle on the ground a few feet away and walked over to stand behind Danny.

"Earl, you push up when I tell you. We're going to get this boy in his saddle."

Earl nodded and grabbed the elbow of Danny's right arm.

Cord lifted Danny's left foot and rammed the toe of his boot into the stirrup. Then he nodded to Earl, lifted Danny up, and shoved him toward the saddle.

"Swing his right leg over the horse," Cord said.

Earl pushed on Danny's right leg until it swung over the horse. Danny sat up straight, his right arm dangling at his side. His left hand gripped the saddle horn.

"There you go, Danny. Now just sit tight while Earl brings our horses over. Then we'll all ride together, down the mountain, and back to your rat's nest of a home."

"Wild, you're twenty kinds of bastard. I'll piss on your grave one day."

"Danny, you're all mouth, and if you don't do what I tell you, I'll crack that other hand with the butt of my pistol."

Danny glared down at him.

"Bring our horses over, Earl," Cord said as he reached for the reins of Danny's horse in his brother's hand.

Earl scrambled off and Cord aimed his pistol at Danny as he stepped back. He pulled hard on the reins and brought the horse's head down.

Danny's left boot twitched.

"You touch a spur to that horse, I'll just shoot you out of the saddle. There's more than one way to deliver a message. It can be done dead or alive."

Danny clamped his lips together. His eyes flashed a look of hatred at Cord.

Earl returned. He led the two horses by the reins.

"Mount up, Earl," Cord said. "And I'll hand you the reins."

A few seconds later, Earl held the reins of Danny's horse while Cord mounted Windmill. Cord took the reins back as he holstered his pistol, thumbing the hammer back to half cock.

"We'll lead out, Earl," Cord said, ticked Windmill's flanks with his spurs, and gave him his head with a loose bit.

They rode down the mountain toward Horace's ranch. They rode slow and gradual as if they were on a Sunday jaunt.

Danny never said a word. He just looked at his shattered gun hand and wept.

TWENTY-THREE

E arl rode up beside Cord when they stopped to rest in the thick timber.

It seemed to him that they had been riding through the roughest timber and brush, and he was tired of looking at the back of Danny and his bloody, mangled hand. Danny kept lifting his hand and stroking his arm as if to ease the pain.

Now their prisoner sat his horse and looked all around at the trees, as if trying to get his bearings.

Or trying to plan an escape.

"Cord, why don't you just shoot this bastard so we can take a nap? Be rid of him." Earl whispered his words so that Danny would not hear him.

Cord took out a rhubarb stalk, wiped it down, and stuck one end in his mouth. His teeth crunched the fibrous stalk. He bit off a portion and chewed it before he spoke.

"It would be wrong to shoot a man who is your prisoner, Earl. Besides, he's going to do some work for us."

"What? Warn Horace that we're coming for him?"

"Make Horace sweat."

"Aw, we should just kill 'em all."

"It might wind up that way," Cord said.

"It might not, too."

"Just let me do this my way, Earl. Remember? I told you that you'd have to follow my orders."

"But we've got one of 'em. And besides, he was tryin' to kill you."

"But he didn't succeed. And now he's disabled and will serve a purpose. My purpose."

"He might try to trick you, Cord."

"He might. I'll still get Horace. He's the leader, the head of the snake. Once you cut off the head, the body dies."

"I get your thinkin', Cord. You got a good brain. I just think it's useless to let this Danny feller live. He's one of them and they don't deserve to live."

"Have some patience, Earl. Rome wasn't built in a day."

Cord smiled. Earl looked puzzled. He had never heard the expression before and he had only a vague notion of what or where Rome was.

"I just think you're wrong to let this thief live when you got him cold. One shot to the head and it's over."

"Back to life and death, are we? Son, you'd better think long and hard about killing another human being."

"I have thought about it."

"Not deep enough, I reckon. You kill a man, it's something you carry with you for the rest of your life."

"It hasn't bothered you none."

Cord stopped chewing and looked at Earl with a stern expression on his face.

"I carry the memory of each man I've had to kill," Cord said. "At the moment of death from my own hand, it's like I've fallen into a deep canyon. It's like the ground gives way under my feet. I hang in midair for a minute and feel all empty inside. Then I fall into a canyon with no bottom. I just fall until I get back my senses."

"God," Earl said.

"I wonder what the dead man's life might have been if I hadn't pulled the trigger," Cord said. "And I wonder where I've sent the man. To hell or to someplace I can't see? Maybe he's gone into nothingness, just wiped out with no body and no brain."

"You think about that stuff a lot?" Earl asked.

"I do. A lot."

"Hmmm. I guess I don't know much."

"You know. You just don't think a lot of things through. Like what Danny means to us at this point. He's a valuable piece of property."

"I guess you're right, Cord."

"So get over it. Don't think about what Danny has done or tried to do to me. Just think of what he's going to do. For us."

"I reckon I can do that."

Cord took another bite of the rhubarb.

"Let's ride on down," he said. "Get this over with."

Earl rode back to where he'd been, behind Danny, as Cord eased Windmill down the slope through the heavy timber.

By late afternoon, at their slow pace, they were near the ranch. Cord led them to the edge of the foothills and halted his horse. He gazed out at the prairie and in the distance he could see the tops of the house and barn.

He looked back at Danny.

Danny glared at him with squinted eyes.

"That's the ranch yonder," Earl said. "Ain't it?"

"There it is," Cord replied.

They rode out onto the plain. Cord didn't want to get too close, where they would be spotted, but he wanted to run Danny's horse up to the house where all could see what had happened to him.

The ranch house began to rise from the plain as they rode closer. Corrals and the barn came into view. And horses.

Earl's eyes narrowed when he saw the horses. Men were herding them to a large grassy enclosure, through a large gate. Poles ringed the enclosure.

"Them are our horses, Cord," Earl exclaimed. "That damned Abner . . ."

"You recognize them?"

"I sure do. Them horses was ours and Abner stole 'em."

"Steady, Earl. Nothing you can do about it just yet."

"Damn," Earl blurted.

Cord turned his horse around and rode up to Danny.

Danny stared at him with his pale eyes.

"You're on your home range, Danny. Time to pay the piper."

"Go to hell, Wild," Danny muttered.

"Maybe you can put some liniment on that hand and start it to healing," Cord said.

"Liniment won't help."

"Soak it in warm water, then."

"I'd like to soak you," Danny said.

"Well, you're going to leave us. And you be sure and tell Horace that he doesn't have long to live."

"We'll hunt you down, Wild, like the dog you are."

"That's fine. Manhunters are my specialty."

Cord leaned over and drew his knife from his scabbard.

He cut the reins of Danny's bridle off at the bit. Danny's face contorted in anger.

Then Cord sheathed his knife and rode to the horse's rear. He doubled up his fist and slammed it onto the horse's rump.

Danny's horse reacted. Its hind legs collapsed and then it leaped forward. It ran off, headed for the ranch house and the other horses. All Danny could do was hang on to his saddle horn with one hand.

Cord turned Windmill and spoke to Earl.

"Let's get out of here," he said, and put spurs into the horse's flanks.

The two rode up into the foothills to the sound of men's shouts as Danny's horse galloped into their midst.

Cord kept riding, with his brother close behind. He did not look back.

When they stopped, back in the timber, both men were panting and the horses were winded.

"Now what?" Earl asked.

"Now we cover our tracks and make a wide circle. We'll come at the ranch from a different direction."

"Won't some of them be huntin' us up here?"

"I don't think so. Not after what happened to Danny. They'll be thinking about defense and they'll have riders out looking for us."

"How will we get to Horace and Abner?"

"I'll give that some thought," Cord said. "And we'll wait until dark to make our move."

Earl looked up at the sky, marked where the sun was blazing across the afternoon in a sea of blue. So long to wait, he thought, and he had no idea of how they would ever get to Horace and Abner. The Weatheralls would lock themselves in their house. And men would be waiting for Cord and Earl, armed to the teeth, ready to shoot on sight or at the slightest sound.

All the odds were against them, Earl thought.

At that moment, everything looked hopeless to him.

And, although Cord's mind was racing, his own thoughts were not far behind.

Everything did look hopeless.

TWENTY-FOUR

Danny's horse trotted into the front yard. All of those nearby saw him, saw the blood and his mangled hand.

Men crowded around him.

Horace and Abner heard the hubbub and emerged from the ranch house.

"What in blazin' hell is goin' on here?" Horace demanded.

Jessup spoke up first.

"Danny here is all shot up," he said.

Horace walked around Danny's horse and saw his right hand, which Danny held up over the pommel.

Horace swore. "How'd that happen, Danny?" he demanded.

"Wild. He plumb busted my gun hand."

"Damn it all. Can't any of you get this man? He's makin' fools of all of us." Horace glared at the men gathered around him and at Abner.

"He don't do anything regular, boss," one of the men said.

"Danny, you put some iodine on your hand. Then maybe we'll get you to a doc. Jessup, help him down out of his saddle."

"Sure," Jessup said and reached up for Danny as the injured man swung his right leg over the pommel.

"Just ease yourself down, Danny," Jessup said. "I'll catch you."

He lifted Danny to the ground. Danny wobbled for a minute or two as a wave of dizziness swept over him.

"Lot of pain?" Jessup asked.

"Plenty," Danny said.

"We'll daub that hole with iodine and then you might wash it clean with alcohol."

Jessup noticed the cut reins on Danny's horse. He let out a cry.

Horace saw it, too. As did Abner.

"Bastard made sure Danny couldn't get away," Horace said.

"That Wild must be some kind of bastard," Abner said.

"He's seven kinds of bastard and a backshooter to boot," Horace said.

"Why did he let you go, Danny?" Horace asked.

Danny drew in a deep breath as he looked at Horace. He gave the impression that he was thinking hard before he answered.

"He give me a message," Danny said.

"Oh yeah? What message?" Horace shot Danny a threatening look.

"I told him I wasn't no messenger and wouldn't deliver it, Horace."

"Well, by God, you will deliver it or I'll have your miserable hide, Danny."

There was no mistaking the threatening look now. Horace looked as if his face would explode in sheer anger.

"Wild said your days were numbered, Horace. He told me to tell you he was comin' for you."

Horace swore a stream of curses at Wild, his parents, and all his kin.

"So, you failed, Danny. You let that bastard Wild get the best of you. You must have had him in close range for him to shoot up your hand. How close was he?"

"Fairly close," Danny said.

"How close?"

"Maybe five or six yards. He's sneaky, I tell you. Didn't make a sound and crept up on me."

Horace looked around at the few remaining men.

"Is there any one of you man enough to go after Wild and kill him?"

No one moved or spoke. Instead, the men turned their heads or bowed them in shame.

"That's what I thought. You're all a bunch of lily-livered swine, not worth the powder to blow you all to hell. I'm disgusted with all of you. And, Danny, you can just pack your duds and ride out of here. I have no use for a man who can't shoot a gun."

"I'll leave, Horace," Danny said, "but you better watch your ass. Wild is coming after you. You can lay good money on that."

Danny walked away, toward the bunkhouse.

"You're going to need another bridle, Danny," Jessup called after him.

"Yeah, yeah," Danny said as he lifted his right hand to acknowledge the advice.

Horace spat onto the ground.

"We got enough men here to make sure Wild can't get to you, Horace," Jessup said.

Abner cleared his throat and spoke up.

"Well, I ain't skeered of that Wild rascal. Just let him try to kill Horace and he'll walk into a hail of hot lead."

"That's the spirit," Jessup said. "Same with the rest of us. I say we'll kill both Wild and his brother, Earl, that snot-nosed kid. Just let 'em try to come here."

"Brave talk," Horace said. "But he doesn't want to kill just me. Each one of you is a marked man in his eyes."

"Don't worry, Horace," Abner said. "We won't let him get close. He comes within rifle range, he's dead meat."

The men all grunted in assent.

"All right, then," Horace said. "From now on, I want each man to carry a rifle or keep one handy while you go about your chores. You look, you listen, and you see anyone ride up here, day or night, you shoot to kill."

The men all nodded.

"And we'll start right away. Wild may be close. He might be watching us right now."

The men dispersed and Abner slapped Horace on the back.

"That's tellin' 'em, Horace. You got men here who will defend you, that's for sure."

Horace looked at Danny's horse, saw the blood spattered on the stirrup and pommel of his saddle.

"I thought Danny could do it," Horace said.

"Well, he made a mistake, that's all."

"There's still Eddie Lomax. I'm countin' on him to kill them two Barnes women so's I can take over the JB Ranch."

"He should be back in the mornin' with the good news," Abner said.

"Let's load up some rifles and find a place where Wild can't see us," Horace said. "Long as it's daylight, we can be on the lookout ourselves."

"Suits me," Abner said. "I'm in the mood for a killin', man or boy."

Horace grinned as the two walked back to the house.

A while later, Danny rode off the ranch, his right hand black with iodine and a towel wrapped around it. He had a bandage on his leg, too, a pair of bandannas that were soon soaked through with more blood.

Unknown to him, Wild's bullet had opened a puncture hole in his femoral artery and he would die before he reached Cheyenne.

He lost consciousness and fell from the saddle. On the ground, he bled to death as he stared at the mountains and longed for their serenity.

TWENTY-FIVE

Ernesto was restless. He couldn't sleep. He kept thinking of Jesse and how he had died. He thought, too, of Abigail and Lelia, alone in that big house without a man. It wasn't fair.

He walked through the stables and into each stall. There, he petted the horses, checked their fetlocks and stroked their withers. He spoke to each one in low tones.

Abigail had told him that they must go over their stock and select the best horses. She wished that he would take a herd of their finest mounts and try to sell them to the army.

"Jesse planned to do that anyway," she said to Ernesto. "We have a mortgage payment due at the bank soon."

That's when a messenger rode up that afternoon and handed her a statement from the bank. It stated that they had sold her mortgage to Horace Weatherall and he was now legally the holder.

"This changes everything," she said.

"It could not be worse," Ernesto said. "Horace will be waiting like the vulture to pounce on you."

"So I must make that next payment, and there's one more after that."

"I will try and sell the horses to the army," Ernesto said. "But after that?"

"I don't know, Ernesto. Jesse would know what to do. We might have enough to buy more horses at the auction in Denver."

"Those are not the best horses sometimes," he said. "Some are wild, others have been misused or mishandled."

"Still, we must raise more cash," she said.

"We might be able to find good horses in Mexico. At very low prices. I would go there and speak to my cousin, Julio Vargas. He catches wild horses and breaks them. He is just over the border."

"That's a long way from here," Abigail said.

"A long ride, yes, but we could add good horses to your stock."

"I'll think about it," she said. "Thanks, Ernesto."

Ernesto thought about the ride to Mexico as he checked each horse in the stable. They had about twenty good horses that the army might buy. After that, they had another dozen or so of breeding stock that would produce in time. Probably not enough to help Abigail save the ranch.

He walked out in back of the stables and found a clear spot, where he rolled a cigarette. He lit a match and smoked as he looked up at the night sky. It was filled with stars, and the Milky Way glowed like a huge band of light.

The night sky gave him comfort. He thought of how far away those stars were and wondered if someone up there was looking down on earth. The universe was a great mystery, but showed the handiwork of a superior mind and perhaps a being that was God. Ernesto was not a religious man, but he believed some superior being had designed the earth and the heavens.

Ernesto was jarred from his celestial reverie by just the tick of a tiny sound.

It wasn't much, the scrape of a boot on stone, a scuff of a heel in the gritty dirt, a toe rolling over a pebble.

Somewhere. Out in front of the house.

A dog? A loose horse?

One of the hands?

Ernesto stood at attention, all of his senses on full alert.

He crept through the barn, a hand on the grip of the converted Remington .44-caliber on his hip, a pistol fully loaded with six bullets.

Eddie Lomax reined his horse to a halt when he saw the glint of moon atop the Barnes ranch house. He ground-tied the black mustang to a bush after he eased slowly out of the saddle. He would not need his rifle, so he left it in its boot.

He walked carefully toward the house, his pistol loose in its holster. He touched the skinning knife on his belt, his fingers tracing the curve of the smooth bone handle, the grooves in its surface. Touched the hilt, and it was cold to his fingertips.

He moved so slowly that he did not disturb or alarm the horses in their pens and corrals. One step, two. Pause. Listen. Another step. Stop, listen. Two more short steps, then listen.

The house was dark, so he knew the occupants, the two women, were in bed. Probably asleep.

More steps.

Too dark to see the ground clearly. His sole disturbed a small round rock. The rock made a sound as it rolled into another.

Eddie cursed silently. He cursed the perversity of inan-
imate objects.

Then he waited for several seconds.

He took another step. Closer to the house. It was almost
in full view.

More careful steps. One step, pause. Another step, pause.
No hurry.

The door would be the challenge. The noise it might
make. Unless it was unlatched.

He prayed that it would be as he took still another careful
and light step. He waited until his weight was fully settled
on the front foot, then raised the other to advance himself.

He listened and heard only the stillness of the night.
Glancing above him, he looked at the silent stars. The blind
stars that could not see him or cry out a warning.

The crease of a smile bent his lips and he took another step.

Closer and closer he came to the front of the house. It,
too, was silent. Silent as a tomb. The tomb it would become.

No front porch. Just a two-tiered wooden step in front of
the door.

His eyes adjusted to the deeper darkness cast by the over-
hanging roof that jutted from the house. A few more steps
and he could make out the door handle, a curved, ornate
iron curlicue that beckoned to him.

He stopped when he came close to the steps. He stood
there and took a deep breath.

And listened.

He leaned over the steps and put an ear to the door. And
listened still more. He heard no sounds from inside the house,
and the crease of a smile broke the plane below his nose.

Somewhere, far off, a horse nickered. A mere wisp of a
sound. Nothing to do with him. A horse ranch would have

such a sound. And other noises as horses moved around in their pens or corrals.

Eddie waited for several moments. He gathered the resolve to try the door handle. He reached down and gripped the handle. He pushed it down and it did not stick.

The door was unlocked.

He stepped up to the first step and then heard the sound of a footfall as Ernesto rounded the corner of the house.

He saw just the dimmest silhouette of a human figure blackened by darkness.

Eddie lifted his boot off the step and turned to face the unwelcome intruder. The fingers of his hand squeezed the grip of his pistol.

Then he saw the man at the corner of the house reach for his pistol and start to pull it from its holster.

A cloud drifted over the moon and deepened the darkness around the house.

Eddie squinted as he snatched his pistol from its leather perch at his side.

Time seemed to freeze in that instant until he heard the man speak.

"What are you doing here?" Ernesto said as his pistol cleared leather.

But the man at the door of the house did not answer. And his arm and hand were moving. There was a pistol in the man's hand and it rose to a deadly level.

TWENTY-SIX

Ernesto squeezed the trigger and felt his pistol buck in his palm.

At the same time, Eddie fired his pistol. At a shadow. At a wavering shadow thirty yards away.

Ernesto's shot went wide of its mark. Eddie's bullet narrowly missed Ernesto.

Ernesto heard it sizzle past his ear in a rush of air. He bent over in a crouch and fired again at the man standing at the doorway of the house. He heard a smack as his bullet tore into human flesh. He fired again, aiming his pistol a little lower in the hopes that the trajectory would elevate the round into the center of the man's body.

He heard a grunt as the bullet smacked home. He saw the man double up.

But Eddie fired again and again, squeezing the trigger

of his double-action Colt until all six cartridges were spent. His shots were true.

Eddie leaned against the wall of the house, blood pouring from his leg and abdomen. He knew that he was mortally wounded. He clutched the wound below his stomach and felt the blood gush. He could smell the scent of his own intestines.

It would be a slow death. Eddie had seen gut-shot men and animals before.

He tried to eject the spent cartridges from his pistol. His fingers were slick with blood and he had trouble pushing the ramrod after he opened the gate, and the cartridge cylinder flipped out of the side of the receiver.

He looked at the man who had shot him, but the figure was a blur as his eyes filled with tears. The pain in his leg and gut was intense. Shoots of agony coursed through his body like waves of electrical shocks.

Ernesto crept forward along the wall of the house. He couldn't remember how many times he had fired, but he thought he had at least two bullets left in the cylinder of his converted Remington. Two .44 slugs left to finish off the intruder.

Eddie slumped down to a sitting position on the top step. He held his gut in, but he still bled with every pump of his heart.

Ernesto put the muzzle of his pistol close to Eddie's temple.

"You do not have long to live. Why did you come here?"

"I ain't sayin', you damned greaser."

Ernesto uttered a wry laugh. "You call me names, but you are the one who is dying."

"I ain't talkin' to no greaser," Eddie said through tight lips.

"Then go to where you belong, gringo. To the grave."

The front window glowed with lamplight from the front room.

Ernesto heard sounds from inside the house: padding feet across the floor, women's voices.

The door opened and Abigail jumped back when she saw the man on her step and Ernesto holding a pistol to his head.

A moment later, Lelia appeared behind her and looked over her shoulder. She gasped and put a hand to her mouth.

"Ernesto. I heard gunfire. Who is this man?" Abigail said as she regained her composure.

"He try to break into the house," Ernesto said. "I do not know who this man is. But he try to shoot me and I shoot him."

"He doesn't look familiar." She turned to Lelia. "Have you ever seen that man before?" she asked.

Lelia shook her head. "He's all bloody," she said. "Oooh, I can't look at him."

She turned away, but Abigail continued to stare down at the bleeding man.

"He's dying, isn't he?" she said to Ernesto.

"Yes, he dies."

"All I can think of is that he was sent here by Horace Weatherall. Probably to kill us so that he could foreclose on our ranch."

Ernesto said nothing, but he mulled over what Abigail had said and nodded his head.

"He is a bad one," Ernesto said.

"You won't . . . have . . . this ranch long, lady," Eddie said in a halting voice.

"You don't know what you're talking about, mister," Abigail said.

"Shoot me, Mex," Eddie said. "Go ahead and get it over with."

"You die slow. You have time to think about your sins, gringo."

Eddie doubled over in pain. He rocked back and forth on the porch. Then he stopped and one of his legs kicked out as a surge of pain struck him in his abdomen. He stifled a cry and Ernesto could hear his teeth rub together.

Ernesto stepped back and eased down the hammer of his pistol. He slid it back in his holster. Then he grabbed Eddie by his shoulders and pulled him off the step and out into the open, where he shoved him down so that the gunman was flat on his back. He searched him to make sure he didn't have a gun.

He turned to the doorway.

"Go back to bed, Abigail," he said. "He will die before morning. No need for you to worry."

"Oh, I don't know if we can sleep after this fight," she said. "But good night, Ernesto. And thank you for saving our lives."

Abigail closed the door.

A moment later, the window went dark as the lamp was extinguished.

The house went silent again as the women returned to their beds.

Ernesto winced as the wounded man's body twisted around in agony. He hated to see anyone, any animal, suffer. But he knew that the man he had shot had come to murder or kidnap Abigail and Lelia. And he knew that Horace had sent him. Horace wanted the JB Ranch. He had bought the mortgage from the bank for just that purpose.

Where was Wild?

Wild would want to know about the mortgage and this man who had sneaked up to do harm to the heirs of Jesse's ranch.

"Kill me, greaser. Shoot me." Eddie croaked the words out. His voice was weak.

Ernesto was tempted.

"You'd shoot a horse with a broken leg, Mex. Do the same for me. Please." The last word from Eddie's mouth sounded pitiful to Ernesto. It tore at his heart and disturbed his conscience. It was not good to let a man suffer like that. But perhaps it was just.

"I will say a prayer for you, gringo. But you must suffer for your sins."

"Crap," Eddie said. "I'm dying. What more do you want?"

"That is enough, gringo. You will die soon."

Eddie moaned in pain.

Less than an hour later, he gave a last gasp. His body spasmed and then he was still. Ernesto leaned down and listened close to the man's mouth. No air was going in or coming out.

He felt a great sense of relief. The stench from the collapsed sphincter muscle assailed his nostrils and he stood upright.

He walked away, toward his quarters. He was tired. He was sleepy.

A bad man was dead.

He crossed himself and said a Hail Mary as he looked up at the stars, the Milky Way.

Was the prayer for himself or for the man he had killed?

Ernesto crossed himself again.

The prayer was for both of them, he decided.

TWENTY-SEVEN

Just before dawn, Ernesto and two other men tied Eddie Lomax's corpse to his horse. They draped the body face-down across the saddle, roped his hands and feet across the horse's belly, and for good measure, tied a length of rope to his belt and looped it beneath the horse.

Ned Parsons tied the last knot.

"Ned," Ernesto said, "you and Pat know what I want you to do?"

Pat Varnum nodded as he held on to the reins of Eddie's horse.

"Yeah, you want me and Pat to tote this horse and dead man over to the 2Bar2 Ranch and run the horse up toward the house."

"Right," Pat said.

"Be real careful. Horace may have riflemen watching for just such a thing." Ernesto breathed a lungful of air.

"We'll watch our topknots, Ernesto," Parsons said.

He turned to his horse and stepped into the stirrup. Then he led Pat's horse over to him and took the reins of Eddie's horse while Pat mounted up and settled into the saddle.

"See you by and by," Pat said to Ernesto.

"If you run into Cord Wild, you tell him to hurry."

"Will do," Pat said.

The two men with their grisly cargo rode off into the dawn.

Ernesto heard the front door creak and turned, walked up to the house.

"Ernesto?" Abigail said.

"Good morning, Abigail. You are up early."

"Couldn't sleep. Are those men taking that dead man somewhere?"

"They'll let Horace know that his little plan did not work."

"Good. But I wish Cord were here. I'd feel safer with a strong man around."

"He will come."

"When?" she asked.

Ernesto shrugged. "Who knows? He comes when he comes."

"That's true," she said. She paused and drew in a breath. "Well, see what stock we can drive to Fort Laramie. We must get some money before we lose everything."

"I will have some horses to sell by nightfall," he said.

The conversation over, Abigail closed the door. Ernesto walked to the stables. He looked to the east and the sky was still dark. Only a little while before sunrise, he knew.

And then there would be a surprise for Horace Weatherall.

Pat and Ned reined their horses to a halt a short distance from the 2Bar2 Ranch.

Two men rode up on either side of them. They rode in out of the dark, pistols shining in their hands.

"Hands up," Cord said.

Both men raised their hands.

Cord rode up and looked at the faces of the two men.

"Pat?"

"Yeah, Cord. It's me and Ned."

"What you got there on the horse you're leading?"

"Dead man," Pat replied. "You still need that gun on us?"

Earl and Cord holstered their pistols.

"Who is he?" Cord asked.

"Don't know," Pat answered. "Ernesto shot him. Said he was tryin' to break into the ranch house."

"What?"

"That's what Ernesto said. The women didn't get hurt, but Ernesto said that's who this one was after, Abigail and Lelia."

"Damn," Cord said. "Mind if I take a look?"

"No, if you can see his face in the dark."

"I'll light a match," Cord said. He rode to the rear, then called to Earl, "Come here, Earl. See if you know this jasper."

Cord struck a match and lifted Eddie's head so that Earl could see his face.

"Yeah, I know who he is," Earl said. "Who he was. Eddie Lomax. One of that bunch that raped our mother and who worked for Abner. A no-account. I'm glad he's dead."

Cord blew the match out.

"You're runnin' the dead man over to the 2Bar2?" Cord rode up to Pat.

"Yeah. Before it gets light, if we can."

"You're almost there. Watch out, though, the spread is bristling with guns."

"We'll turn this horse loose the first chance we get."

"You'd better," Cord said.

"Ernesto said if we run into you to have you skedaddle back to the JB."

"We'll wear out leather getting back," Cord said, and turned Windmill. He and Earl rode off toward the JB, horses at a gallop.

A half hour later, a rent opened in the eastern horizon and spilled creamy light through its fissure.

Cord was glad that he had decided to ride back to the JB before going after Horace.

Weatherall had stepped over a line in the sand by sending a gunman to kill or kidnap Abigail and Lelia. Cord was more determined than ever to put Horace's lamp out and clean out the whole rat's nest at the 2Bar2.

Horace had gone far enough. In fact, he had gone too far.

TWENTY-EIGHT

Lelia rushed into Cord's arms the minute he stepped across the threshold of the ranch house. Nearly knocked him back through the door.

Earl's eyes went wide as he stepped up just behind his brother.

"Oh, thank God you're here, Cord," Abigail exclaimed.

Cord pulled Lelia's arms down from around his neck.

"Wish I had come sooner," he said.

Lelia glided away to stand by her mother. Ernesto walked into the room with a tray of coffee cups. He wore a large grin as he set the tray down on a small table in front of the divan.

"Thank you, Ernesto," Abigail said. "Let's all sit down and have some hot coffee before our hearts fly out of our chests," she said.

Ernesto slapped Cord on the back. "Much to tell," he said.

"Ernesto's right," Abigail said as all the men sat down in chairs except for Cord, who joined the two women on the divan after Abigail patted a place between her and Lelia.

Ernesto handed cups of coffee to all who were there and took one for himself.

"I saw the hands packing the body of the man you shot, Ernesto," Cord said. "I'd like to hear just what happened last night."

"Yes, go ahead, Ernesto," Abigail said. "Tell Cord what happened. How you saved our lives."

Ernesto told Cord the full story of his encounter with Eddie Lomax.

"It was frightening," Abigail said. "I heard those gunshots outside and thought we were under attack."

"I was petrified," Lelia said.

"You're lucky that Ernesto was here to defend you," Cord said.

"What will happen to us?" Abigail asked.

"If Horace is killed, he can't foreclose on the JB Ranch," Cord said. "You won't lose it."

"But how? How can you get to that monster?" Abigail asked.

"There's always a way," Cord said.

"What will you do?" Lelia asked.

"There are several ways we can get to him. I'm just sorting through the possibilities," Cord said.

Earl gave him a questioning look. So did Lelia.

"I'll find a way," Cord said. "His time on this earth is drawing to a close."

It was true. Cord was considering several ways to get at Horace and his brother. He had no qualms about killing men who had already shown their murderous ways. He knew that the law couldn't touch him at this point. There was probably no law outside of Cheyenne, and even that law was pretty weak.

No, this was something he would have to do for himself. He and Earl. He knew they would be facing a formidable opponent. A wily adversary, at that. Horace was cagey and he surrounded himself with top gunmen, men who had killed beforc and would not hesitate to defend their evil boss.

"I hope you can do this, Cord," Abigail said.

"I'll do it," Cord said.

Abigail rose from the divan.

"I'll fix all of us breakfast. Lelia, you can help. First, go to the henhouse and fetch me some eggs."

Lelia jumped up from the couch with alacrity and dashed down the hall to the kitchen and back door.

Ernesto sat there and looked at Cord.

"Do you want me to go with you when you go after Horace?" he asked.

Cord thought about it. There was no doubt that Ernesto was eager to go after Horace and the other men on the 2Bar2, and it's possible one more man could add to their chances of success, but Ernesto might also get in the way. Cord did not think he had the experience to stalk and kill a man.

Yes, he had defended the women here, but that did not add much to his experience or capability. He had blood on his gun, but not much else.

"Ernesto," Cord finally replied, "I appreciate your offer. But I think you can do more good staying here on the JB. No telling if, or when, Horace will try again to murder or kidnap the women. You can be here to defend them while my brother and I go after the snakes on the 2Bar2."

"Okay. I will protect the women with my life."

Cord sensed that Ernesto was relieved to stay on the ranch.

After a hearty breakfast, Cord walked outside to be by himself. He had left Earl to dry the dishes that Lelia washed, while Abigail changed into riding togs to inspect the stock.

Cord walked over to the trees where Danny had gotten his messages from Horace, which Ernesto had told him about.

He knew how hard it would be to get at Horace. Should he find a way to lure him into the open and try a long rifle shot to end his life? Or should he just kill all his men, one by one, until only Horace and Abner were left to defend themselves?

He puzzled over different scenarios for a long time.

Until he thought of a plan that suited him. Yes, it was a difficult plan, but it should work. It would require perfect timing, stealth, and careful attention to detail. It was risky, but so were the other methods he had considered.

One thing was certain, Cord thought. Horace and his cohorts must be sent to their deaths. They had proven that they did not respect the lives of others. They were all born killers, to Cord's way of thinking.

None of them deserved to live.

But could he live with what he had to do? Human life was precious to him. Not only his life, but the lives of others.

He had had his fill of killing after shooting the two horse thieves. Yes, they had tried to kill him, but was that reason enough to kill them? Cord wrestled with his conscience and he wrestled with his own morality.

There was an unwritten law in the West. Horse thieves could be killed when caught red-handed. Hanged or shot, it made no difference.

But was there a morality to the law? For a law without morality was not worth the paper it was written on. He knew that much.

The horse was the mainstay of the ranching business. It was a most valuable commodity in the West. Lives depended on the horse. So did livelihoods. When a horse was stolen, a family could starve to death or go bankrupt. A lone man could die from heat or thirst if left afoot in a dangerous place.

So a horse thief was among the most hated of criminals.

And horse thieves deserved to die.

That was how serious it was, Cord decided.

And Horace and his bunch were proven horse thieves. They were a scourge of the Great Plains.

Out here, on this great expanse of land, there was no law.

So when a man encountered a horse thief, he became the law.

Cord's conscience was clear. He had, in his mind, become the law. He had become justice itself against a band of men who had no sense of either the law or morality.

Therefore, they all must die.

And, Cord resolved, they all must die in the worst way possible.

TWENTY-NINE

N estor Jones grumbled as he stepped down into the hole he and Pete Gander had dug. He shoveled a pile of dirt from the two-foot-deep grave.

"This here ranch is gettin' to be a graveyard," he said.

Pete was making one side of the grave smooth by shoveling straight down. He flung the dirt into a pile alongside the cavity.

"We never really got to know that feller who lies yonder," he said.

Both men stopped for a minute, the blades of their shovels coming to a halt. They both looked over at the body of Eddie Lomax a few feet away.

"He was supposed to be a top gun," Nestor said.

"Haw. Got hisself shot dead, he did. Some kind of top gun, you ask me."

Nestor leaned on his shovel handle and looked over at

Pete. "I'm thinkin' this card game is over, Pete. Look at how many graves is dug here. How many men six feet under."

"Gets worse ever' day," Pete said. "Horace is havin' fits over losin' so many men in such a short time. Either run off or killed."

"It's that damned Wild, the one they call the Wild Gun. He ain't natural, you ask me. Ain't nobody come close to puttin' his lamp out. No matter who Horace sends out to kill him, he sends 'em back dead or as good as."

"No, it don't seem natural to me, either. Man can't live a charmed life forever."

"But Wild don't go down. No matter who gives it a try."

"That's true. I think Horace is runnin' out of ideas about how to stop Wild."

"What if he sends you to track Wild down? Would you go, Pete?"

Pete shook his head. "I ain't no tracker, and it would be like a death sentence."

"Same here," Nestor said. "Horace tells me to chase down Wild, I'd light a shuck twixt me and him."

"But you'll stand guard, Nestor."

"Maybe."

"What do you mean, 'maybe'? Horace would shoot you down if you refused."

"I guess I'll stand guard. Up to a point."

"What point?"

"Until I got shot at, I reckon."

Pete lifted his shovel and began to scrape the dirt wall of the grave again.

Nestor raised his own shovel but looked off in the distance. "Rider comin' this way," he said.

Pete looked over his shoulder. "That's Jessup. He's on the lookout for Wild like all of us are." He looked over at their rifles, which were leaning against a tree a few yards away where the horses were ground-tied to brush.

"Checkin' on us, likely," Nestor said.

"I'll be glad when this damned grave is done and Eddie is planted. Gives me the willies."

Nestor laughed and lifted a shovelful of dirt from the grave. He upended the shovel and dirt fell on the pile he was building.

Jessup rode up. "How you comin'?" he asked.

"We're diggin'," Nestor said.

"Horace wants you to hurry it up. He wants as many men on guard as he can get, just in case Wild makes a move on his promise."

"We've got a ways to go," Pete said.

"Horace said the grave don't have to be deep. Just so's Eddie's underground."

"How deep, then?" Pete asked.

"No more'n two feet, Horace says."

"Coyotes or wolves will dig him up," Nestor said.

"Horace don't care." Jessup looked around at the bleak and empty landscape. There wasn't an antelope in sight, or anything else that he could see. This gave him a creepy feeling, as if someone was watching him from afar.

The hairs on the back of his neck seemed to crawl up into his scalp. The hairs stiffened, and he lifted his rifle an inch or two off the pommel. He slid a hand onto his shirt and felt the contours of the binoculars that dangled from his neck on a strap. He lifted the binoculars to his face and adjusted them over his eyes. He scanned the distant reaches of the prairie and turned the center knob to bring everything into focus at around three hundred yards.

He moved the binoculars slowly from left to right while his right finger poked inside the trigger guard of his rifle.

Just in case, he thought.

In case he saw a rider heading his way. Wild, maybe. Or that kid brother of his. Then he saw something move, and halted the scan with the binoculars.

There it was again.

Movement. An animal, or a man on his knees, moved a few feet, then stopped.

Jessup strained his eyes to make out just what it was that he saw through the lenses of the binoculars.

Pete and Nestor stopped shoveling. They looked up at Jessup on his horse. They sensed that he saw something with those glasses.

Pete's lips dried out and he slid a wet tongue over them. Nestor swallowed and his Adam's apple bobbed against the taut skin of his neck.

Neither man spoke.

Jessup's head did not move as he stayed fixed on what he saw in the distance. Whatever or whoever it was had stopped, and he saw just the barest outline of something that was not grass or dirt.

A moment or two later, Jessup relaxed and his hackles softened. His breath was a long sigh of relief as a coyote trotted into view, a jackrabbit dangling from its jaws.

"Only a coyote," Jessup said to the two gravediggers.

"Boy, you're sure jumpy," Pete cracked.

"You try guardin', Pete. It ain't easy. Wild could come from anywhere, and I don't fancy gettin' shot out of the saddle by someone I can't see."

"Aw, I was just joshin', Jessup. I know it ain't easy."

"When you finish plantin' Lomax, you two are wanted back at the ranch house. Horace has something in his craw again."

"Well, we ain't goin' into them mountains after Wild. I'll tell you that," Nestor said.

"He doesn't want you to go after Wild," Jessup said. "I think he wants you to dig some holes with them shovels."

"Dig some holes?" Pete exclaimed. "What for?"

"Like in the war," Jessup said. "Holes what can hide a rifleman."

Both Pete and Nestor snorted. Then they began to shovel dirt again.

Jessup rode off and made a half circle before riding back on his rounds.

By then, the grave was dug and he saw only a mound of dirt where the grave had been. And the other mounds that told the story of men no longer among the living.

The day wore on and the silence of the prairie was deafening.

Jessup scanned the empty landscape as if Wild would magically appear and ride within range of his rifle.

Fat chance, Jessup thought.

THIRTY

Harley Davis stood guard near the front door of Horace's house. He walked back and forth, rifle held across his chest. He looked nervously toward the open prairie. He stopped his pacing when he saw two riders emerge on the horizon. He shaded his eyes to bring them into focus under the harsh light of the morning sun. His right hand index finger stroked the trigger guard of his Winchester .30-30.

As they drew closer, he saw shovels sticking out on both sides of their cantles and recognized Pete Gander and Nestor Jones. He knew they were returning from the place where they had buried Lomax. They both looked tired, and both slumped in their saddles as they rode straight toward the house.

He watched as they both reined up at the hitch rail and dismounted.

"Horace in there?" Pete asked Davis.

"Him and his brother are both inside," Davis replied. "So what?"

"Jessup said Horace wanted to see us," Nestor said.

"He didn't say nothin' to me about wantin' to see you," Davis said.

"Somethin' about digging holes," Pete added.

Davis snorted. "Somebody's pullin' your leg, Pete," Davis said.

"At least tell him we're out here," Pete said, annoyed at Davis.

"Horace don't like to be disturbed. Him and his brother are talkin' in there. I'm standin' guard."

"What do you expect, Davis? That Wild is going to just ride up here and start shootin'?"

"I got my orders," Davis said. "I'm standin' guard."

"Unless you want that rifle shoved up your sorry ass, Davis, you'll knock on that there door and tell Horace we're here."

"Why you . . . I ought to . . ."

"Shut up and do what he says, Davis," Nestor said. He took a step toward Davis and dropped his right hand to the butt of his pistol.

Davis snorted again, then turned toward the door. He raised his hand and tapped lightly on the front door, then stepped aside.

Abner opened the door a crack and peeked out.

"What is it?" he asked.

"Fellers here say Horace wanted to see 'em."

Abner opened the door wider and looked at Nestor and Pete.

"Just a minute," Abner said and closed the door. A moment later, he opened it wide.

"You boys come on in," he said.

Pete and Nestor entered the house. Horace stood in front of a window with a yardstick. He held it up to the window, then wrote down some figures in a notebook.

"You wanted us to dig some holes?" Nestor said to Horace.

"Dig some holes? Whatever in hell for?"

"I dunno. Jessup said . . ."

"Jessup hasn't brains enough to sneeze when his nose tickles," Horace said. "To hell with Jessup. I want you boys to go out in back of the barn and start sawin' up boards. Get the sawhorses out of the barn. I got some measurements here."

"Yes, sir," Davis said. "What's the boards for?"

"Boardin' up these winders," Horace said. "So's the Wild Gun can't shoot in here."

"Good idea," Nestor said.

Abner looked on, a blank expression on his face.

"Lot of boards," Nestor said.

"And you boys are going to help me nail them up."

"We'll get on it right away," Pete said.

"One more winder to go," Horace said. "Then I'll give you the list of measurements. And there's a keg of twenty-penny nails out in the barn. Bring those and a couple of hammers when you finish cuttin'."

Both Nestor and Pete nodded. They watched as Horace went to another window with his yardstick. They watched him measure the width of the window on both sides of its frame. They saw him scribble the figure in a small notebook.

When he was finished measuring the last window, Horace tore off three sheets of notepaper and handed them to Nestor.

He and Pete turned and walked to the door, and Abner followed them, then closed the door behind them and locked it.

Horace sat down in his chair. Abner sat down on the divan.

"You think them boards will be enough, Horace?" Abner asked.

"At least Wild won't be able to see us. We'll barricade the front door tonight. I measured the back door, and we'll board that up, too."

"Good idea," Abner said. He pulled a plug of tobacco from his shirt pocket and bit off a small piece. He slid the plug back in his pocket and worried the bitten piece around in his mouth until he found just the right spot between his teeth to bite into it.

"I'm wondering about the men you're going to put on guard tonight," Abner said as he squirted juice to the other side of his mouth.

"What about 'em?"

"They'll get sleepy. Drop their guard. They don't look all that spry to me."

"The reward money will keep them spry enough," Horace said.

"Well, maybe. I just hope we can get some shut-eye tonight."

"With us boarded up, we ought to sleep without no worries, Ab. Just keep a pistol handy. First sound of gunfire, we go after that bastard Wild."

"I just wish we didn't have to worry about Wild," Abner said.

"When he makes his move, it'll be all over. We have enough guns for both him and that snot-nosed little brother of his."

Abner moved the brass spittoon over next to the couch, between his boots, and spat.

Horace listened to the sound of a horse's whinny and smiled.

He'd show Wild. The man didn't stand a chance against

his guns. And he'd find no target in the Weatherall ranch house.

Out by the barn, Pete and Nestor pulled the tarp off one stack of lumber. The tarp covered the two-by-fours. After they picked up the boards they needed, they replaced the tarp and went to the next stack. Underneath, they saw one-by-sixes and left that tarp to lie alongside.

Inside the barn, they found four sawhorses stacked against one wall. In the tack room, they took down two hammers and filled an empty can with nails.

They set up the sawhorses and started lifting the eight-foot boards onto them.

"We got no way to measure these boards," Nestor said as he looked at the list of measurements Horace had given him.

"We got to look in that tack room and find a yardstick," Pete said.

"You go on, Pete," Nestor said. "I'll use my hands to measure the first one."

While Pete was back in the barn, Nestor laid the flat of his hand at the end of one board. He figured the span of it, at its center, to be around four inches. He walked his hand across the board, then notched the spot with one of the saws. He began to saw the board to the length of one of the measurements.

He finished just as Pete emerged from the barn carrying an old yardstick that was stained with tobacco juice, sweat, and oil from lumber.

"Here, measure this one I just cut," Nestor said and laid it across the sawhorse.

"Four feet, two inches," Pete said as he peered down at the numbers on the stick.

Nestor looked at the notepaper.

"Four feet one inch," he said. "Close enough."

"You better hope," Pete said. "This lumber was brung here to build a cookhouse."

"Or another bunkhouse. Horace, he has big dreams."

"I know," Pete said. "He wants to be king of the whole prairie."

"And he's got a whole lot of hate in him, too," Nestor said.

"For Wild, at least."

"For most people," Nestor said. "You can almost feel the hate in him."

Nestor placed the already cut board atop the longer one to make the next measurement. He and Pete continued to do this with all the boards that were the same size for one of the windows. This made the work go faster. Soon, they had several piles of cut boards.

"That's the last one, I think," Pete said as a board fell from the sawhorse.

"I got one more to cut," Nestor said, and the smell of wood tickled his nostrils as the saw gnawed at the board with the sound of a large insect. The board clacked to the ground and he laid his saw down to pick it up.

"We'll have to make several trips," Pete said. "On the last one, we'll take Horace a bucket of nails."

They loaded up their arms with sawed boards and lugged them to the house.

Abner let them in.

"Just set the boards in the center of the front room," he said. "I know you got more to bring."

"Yep," Nestor said.

There was no sign of Horace, but they heard footsteps on the upstairs floor.

When they finished carrying wood slats to the house and brought in a large coffee can full of nails, Horace came downstairs.

"Pete, you come with me," Horace said. "Got your hammer?"

"Right here," Pete said. He reached behind him and pulled a hammer from under his belt.

"We'll start upstairs," Horace told Pete. "Abner, you and Nestor can start with the back door and kitchen."

"Got it," Abner said.

By dusk, the windows in the ranch house were all boarded up, and the back door as well. Horace surveyed all the windows and dismissed the two helpers.

Then he and Abner lifted the couch and set it against the front door. They put an overstuffed chair on top of the couch. Anyone trying to break in through that door would have to move two heavy objects. That would give him and Abner time to aim their rifles and pistols at the intruder and kill him.

"Well, now let the Wild Gun try and get to me," Horace said to his brother.

"He can't get in, and he can't see us. At least not tonight."

"My men will shoot him before he even gets near the house," Horace said.

"Let's hope," Abner said.

"Let's count on it, Ab."

Horace smiled in satisfaction.

THIRTY-ONE

Cord and Abigail stayed up late. They talked in the small parlor after Earl and Lelia went to bed.

Abigail had kept her eyes on Cord all evening. She had been thinking about how they had met, and how much he had done for her husband, Jesse. She realized that she had been wrong about him and wanted to make it right.

"Cord, when this is over, all this horrible business with Horace Weatherall and his brother, I'm going to need a good foreman to run the JB Ranch. Ray Dobbs moved on to another ranch."

"You'll find one," he said.

He sat in an easy chair, the dregs of a coffee on a small table next to him, along with a snifter of brandy. Abigail was in a cushioned straight-backed chair that had belonged to her mother. She, too, had been sipping Jesse's good brandy. It seemed the time to enjoy some spirits after the

sumptuous meal that she and Lelia had prepared: roast
chicken, dumplings, potatoes, and sugar beets.

"I'd want you to run the ranch," she said. "You've done
so much for us, but I don't think you like your life much.
You live alone and you live the life of a hired gun. Nothing
but trouble."

"A man in trouble rides a lonesome trail," he admitted.
"I don't like my life now much."

"But you like horses. Your family raised horses. I got
that much tonight after listening to your brother, Earl."

"It was a good life, growing up in Missouri. Raising
horses. But we dealt with horse thieves back then, too. I
developed an aversion to them."

"I'm serious," she said. "You have more than an aversion
to horse thieves. They've changed your life. I'm offering
you a chance to give up that life and go back to one that was
more like the one you lived in childhood."

Cord raised his head and stared at the ceiling. It was
shadowy with lamplight, beamed and plain like the parlor
his mother had furnished back home. The wooden beams
had been stained a brown color and gave him a feeling of
solid stability. There were Currier & Ives prints in frames
on the wall, a Chinese vase with flowers, and bookshelves
with leather-bound classics that he knew Jesse read, because
he'd often talked about them.

He had not thought about his childhood or the home in
Missouri much lately. Had been deliberately not thinking
of it while he focused on bringing justice to his parents'
killers. But Abigail had stirred memories of the life he once
had. He remembered being with his pa in the stables when
one of the mares delivered a foal. How he had laughed to
see the little creature stand on wobbly legs and flick its little
tail, glad to be alive. He had laughed, too, when the foal

staggered to its mother's teats and found nourishment in the milk it sucked from her full bag.

Then, during the war, rebels had raided their place. Confederates had stolen their grain and hay, and their horses, and ridden down to Arkansas. He had been a callow boy then, but he'd hunted the raiders down, shot them with a .38-caliber Colt cap and ball pistol and an old flintlock his pa had bought from a Kentucky gunsmith.

He had been too young to join the Union Army, but from then on, he'd kept his eyes open for men in Confederate uniforms and had driven them off, with his pa's able help, whenever they came near the farm.

The horses they raised were an integral part of their lives. His ma hand-fed the foals when their mothers were foundering or had died during the birth process. Earl had always put fresh straw in the stalls when a foal was born, had curried and combed the little ones as if they were full-grown.

"You would be paid, Cord," Abigail went on. "Forty a month and found. As our fortunes increased, under your capable hands, I'd raise that to fifty a month."

"That's mighty generous of you, Abigail," he said as he lowered his gaze from the ceiling to her.

"Will you accept my offer?" she asked.

He made a church steeple with his fingers as he considered Abigail's offer.

It would mean giving up some of his freedom, of course. Working on the JB Ranch would also mean that he would work with horses again. More than that, it would mean he would no longer have to hunt down and kill armed thieves on a regular basis. The latter appealed to him. He was sick of killing. Sick of men who stole from others. Sick of murderers.

"I'll consider your kind offer, Abigail. I admit that it appeals to me."

"Down deep, you're a decent man, Cord. I realize that now. You have helped me and Jesse more than you know. We are not used to being trespassed on and robbed, and you made everything right. I just wish we could be left alone to earn our living and do what we love to do in this life."

"You deserve to live a life free of predatory men such as that banker who sold you out."

"Yes, that was not very nice of him," she said.

"It was criminal, Abigail. The bank gave you a loan and that loan obligated it to help protect your interests. Instead, the banker succumbed to greed and sold what was in his keeping to a man who meant to take everything away from you."

"Yes, you're right, Cord. I never thought of it that way. I assumed that the bank would protect my interests and let me repay the loan. It seemed a benefactor at the time. When we needed money to buy stock and work the ranch, they seemed kindly disposed to us."

"That's the way of the world, Abigail. Greed is what built civilization, including towns, laws, authority, and all that assured profits for certain people. And politics reared its ugly head to ensure that the rich got richer and the poor got poorer."

"But without civilization and laws, we'd just be savages," she said.

"We are savages. Civilization has attempted to make us into good citizens. But only with words on a piece of paper. Civilization has nurtured man's greed. It wears a nice-looking suit of clothes, but the person wearing that suit is hiding a knife behind his back."

"You have a very low opinion of both civilization and man's progress from the Stone Age."

"We humans have progressed very little since the Stone Age," he said. "All we did was learn to make clothes and wear them. The greed—for another man's possessions, another man's wife, his tools, his money—remains."

She shuddered in mock fright.

"You're a pessimist," she said. "You look at people as if they were no better than animals. Most people are kind and do not covet other men's wives or possessions."

"Some people have morals, that's true," he said. "Most, deep down, want what others have, and they will go to any lengths to possess what they can."

She let out a breathy sigh.

"I grant you, there is greed in the world, and most people, especially townspeople, are out to get rich, sometimes at other people's expense."

"Take the War Between the States, for instance," he said. "Where families and neighbors fought against each other. There were a lot of people killed in that war, and the politicians in Washington never explained why there was a war in the first place."

"Why, the war was over the abolition of slavery. The South didn't like it."

"The war wasn't over slavery, Abigail."

She lifted her snifter and took a sip of brandy.

"I thought it was," she said.

"The war was about money. It was about cotton crops and profits. Slaveholders didn't have to pay their pickers, their plantation workers. They saw all that money going away and seceded from the Union. That's what the war was about: profit."

"I see your point," she said. "It was about slaves, but it was also about the huge loss of money the South would experience without all that free or cheap help."

Cord drank from his glass and stretched out his legs.

"Our so-called Civil War was one of the bloodiest in history."

Abigail's jaw dropped and her mouth opened in surprise.

"Why, Cord, I think you're right. Our war was not over religion but over . . ."

"Slavery and greed. Look what happened after the war when the carpetbaggers invaded the South. They kicked you when you were down. Made money over other people's misfortune and grief."

Abigail nodded in agreement.

"You're right, of course. I just never thought about the war that way. Or people. Greedy people."

"Just look at Horace, your neighbor, if you want to see greed in action. He's a prime example of what's wrong and immoral in the world."

She sighed and smacked her lips. Then she drained her glass of brandy and stood up.

"Cord, you've given me a lot to think about. I'm tired and going to bed. What do you plan to do tomorrow?"

"I want to get some things together," he said. "I'll be here tomorrow, but Earl and I will ride out tomorrow night."

"You're going after Horace, then?"

"Yes," he said.

He did not finish his brandy, but arose from his chair.

"Thanks for the bed and board," he said. "I'll see you in the morning."

"Good night, Cord."

"Good night, Abigail."

He watched her leave the parlor, then walked to the front door and opened it. He stepped outside and breathed deeply of the cool air.

There was a lot he had to do. He thought that he and Earl could do some damage to Horace and his minions. It would not be easy and his plan might fail.

But for the moment, he was confident. It was all a matter of timing and luck. Good luck.

And then, too, there was the element of surprise.

Horace might never know what hit him.

THIRTY-TWO

Just past midnight, Cord got out of bed. He strapped on his gun belt and tiptoed out of the house. He did not awaken Earl. He wanted his brother sharp and bushy-tailed when they left for the 2Bar2 Ranch. And they would leave soon, when it was full dark and they could not be easily seen.

He was in a downstairs bedroom, next to where Earl slept. The women were asleep upstairs. He opened the door of his room slowly and stepped lightly into the hallway.

He listened to see if he had disturbed anyone, either upstairs or downstairs. The house was quiet. It creaked as the temperature outside dropped.

He tiptoed down the hall toward the kitchen and back porch. He knew he would find what he was looking for in both places.

He entered the kitchen, with its polished wooden flooring, and walked to the counter. There were cabinets above and below. He opened one of the lower cabinets. It was so dark he could not see inside.

Moonlight glazed the windows and filtered through the glass, drenching parts of the room with light that did not illuminate any of the cabinet interiors.

He stuck a hand inside the cabinet and felt around. He struck a small pot and it made a metallic sound as it slid off another pot. Cord winced at making even that small noise.

He closed the cabinet and opened the one next to it. Again, he felt around inside and touched a box and a round tin. His fingers crawled around the bottom, but he kept touching wood or metal. Then he felt a light touch on his shoulder. From where he squatted, he turned and looked up. He saw a face there, blanched by moonlight streaming through the window.

It was Lelia.

She smiled wanly at him and he stood up.

"What are you looking for?" she whispered. She wore a dark chemise and smelled of some kind of flowery perfume.

"Rags," he told her.

He heard a soft titter escape her lips. Saw her white teeth flash as she smiled.

"Wrong cabinets," she said and tugged on his arm. She led him across the kitchen to an oblong box standing on its end. It had a wooden lid on it.

Cord could not read the lettering stamped on the side of the box, but figured it had once held curtain rods or perhaps fireplace pokers.

Lelia reached inside and pulled out a bundle of cloth. She held the mass in front of Cord. "Is this what you're looking for?"

"What are they?" he whispered.

"Flour and bean sacks. We keep them in here for when we have to scrub something awful and ugly."

"That's exactly what I'm looking for," he said and grabbed the sacks from her hands.

"More?" she asked.

He nodded.

She leaned over and pulled still more sacks from the box. "That enough?" she asked. "There's plenty more in the box."

"That's enough," he said.

She watched as he laid the empty sacks on the counter. He flattened them and stacked them into small piles.

When he was finished, he began to fold one of the stacks. Then he stuffed the folded sacks into one of his pants pockets as Lelia looked on. Moonlight dusted one side of her face as she stood at the counter, next to a window. She looked, he thought, like a painted harlequin.

"What do you need all these sacks for?" she whispered.

"Something real important," he said. And that was all he said to her as he continued to pack folded sacks into both back pockets and the front pockets. The last stack sat there for a minute or two.

He unbuttoned his shirt and slid the folded cloth inside and under his belt. He buttoned the shirt and stepped away from the counter.

He looked at Lelia. She was beautiful in the soft glow of moonlight. A beam glanced off her eyes and they looked like shining agates.

"Is that all?" she asked, her voice pitched low and barely above a whisper.

"No. Now I need some old bottles or small jars. Do you have any of those?"

"We keep a barrel next to the back door, outside," she said.

"I need some with lids or corks."

There was the light titter again.

"You probably need another sack to carry them in if you want more than one."

"I do," he said, with a nod of his head.

Lelia went back to the oblong box and rummaged inside. She brought up a large feed sack and held it up so Cord could see its size.

"Perfect," he said.

"Just one?"

"One's enough."

"Whatever are you up to, Cord?" she said as she handed him the sack. "Some deviltry?"

"Deviltry is the word," he said. He followed her to the back door and they both stepped outside.

She stopped and he saw that she had begun to shiver.

The air was chill and the moonlight shining on her chemise gave her the look of an orphaned waif.

"You're cold," he said. "You'd better go back inside. I can get what I need."

There were two barrels on either side of the steps.

She shook her head. "No, I want to help you. Besides, you'll make too much noise and wake up the whole house."

"I'll be careful and quiet," he said.

"I'm not that cold," she said and walked to the barrel on the left of the steps to the back porch.

She lifted the lid and Cord began to sort through the bottles. He chose only those with corks that were thin and held about a quart each. He removed eight bottles from the barrel and then closed the lid.

"What are those for?" Lelia asked.

"Now I need to steal some of your coal oil," he replied.

"Oh. We keep that in the storm cellar. Right over there." She pointed to a slanted board door.

The door creaked slightly when he opened it.

"You'll have to grope your way in the dark," she whispered to him. "You can't light a match in there."

"No, I wouldn't think so," he said. "Bottles?"

"Yes. And in cans. Just to your right when you go down the steps. I'll wait up here and you can hand me a can or a bottle."

He descended the stairs into the dank cellar. It was pitch-dark and he could not see anything that was inside. He groped along the right wall. He felt the bottles, two of them, and then a can with a pouring spout. He lifted the can. It was full and would suit his purpose. He judged it to hold at least three gallons.

He carried the can up the steps and handed it to Lelia. It sloshed when she took it in both hands.

"Now comes the hard part," he said. "I wish I had a funnel."

"We have a funnel," she said. "It's in the house. I'll get it."

She went back into the house and returned a few minutes later with a small funnel that was used to fill the lamps with coal oil.

"Thanks," he said and took the funnel from her. He poured coal oil into each of the bottles and pressed the corks tight. The smell was overpowering and both of them turned their heads to escape the fumes.

When he finished, there was very little oil left in the can.

"Just leave it here," she said. "We'll refill it the next time we go into town for supplies."

"I'll pay you for the oil," he said.

"No you won't. But what is it for?"

"A surprise," he said. "Now to the tack room and my saddlebags."

They walked to the barn. Lelia carried four bottles, Cord the other four. He set the bottles down and entered the dark barn. He found the tack room and entered it. He retrieved his saddlebags and carried them outside to where Lelia waited, her bottles lying at her feet.

Cord hunkered down and began to remove the cloth sacks from his pockets. He put four bottles in one of his saddlebags and packed the sacks around them. Then he put the other four bottles in the other bag and did the same.

"That ought to hold them," he said as he stood up.

"At least the bottles won't break," she said. She felt in each bag and found that the bottles were swathed in cloth. They would not clank or break.

"We'll leave the bags here while I wake up Earl. Then we'll saddle up and be on our way."

"You're going after Horace?" she asked.

"Wish me luck."

She embraced him and held him tight.

"Be careful, Cord," she said. "I don't know what you're going to do, but I know it will be dangerous."

"It will be thorough," he said cryptically as they walked back to the house through a pale haze of moonlight. The smell of coal oil was still cloying in his nostrils.

Lelia shivered against him in the chill of night.

There was plenty of time, he thought, as he looked up at the star-strewn sky, the band of light that was the Milky Way, and the moon inching across a clear sky.

Not an ideal night to do what he had to do. But a good enough night for all hell to break loose.

All hell.

THIRTY-THREE

Earl rubbed his eyes as he saddled Louie in the dark. He was still sleepy and not entirely sure what Cord had in mind for this late-night ride. Lelia had gone back to bed and they were alone outside the barn.

Cord slid his rifle into its scabbard, checked the two cinches under Windmill's belly. He could not slide his fingers between the cinch and the horse. He pressed his hand against both saddlebags as he secured them to the horse's rump. They made no noise. He still had some sacks in his back pockets and he tapped those to make sure they were still secure.

Then he tapped one of his shirt pockets to make sure the matchbox was there. He pulled a fresh rhubarb stalk out of the other pocket and began to chomp it before he stepped up into the saddle.

"Ready, Earl?" he said.

"Just about."

Ernesto appeared out of the darkness, a dim figure drenched in the soft light of the moon.

"You go to the 2Bar2?" he asked.

"You keep an eye out, Ernesto," Cord said. "If we don't come back, say a prayer for us."

"You will be back," Ernesto said.

"I only live in this one moment, Ernesto," Cord said. "The past is gone forever. The future is not yet here. All we can do is just live right now."

"But you are strong, Cord. Horace is weak. He has many men who kill for him, but he is nothing but a cockroach."

Cord chuckled.

"Well, if he's a cockroach, he's going to feel my foot come down on him."

"You will squash him, no?" Ernesto said.

"As long as I have a foot, Ernesto, I will squash Horace."

Ernesto laughed. "And I will piss on his grave," he said.

Cord raised a hand to Ernesto and spurred Windmill. He and Earl rode through the dark toward their destination. The horses glistened a dull gloss of silver in the moonlight. The prairie was a dull pewter filled with shadows that dotted the eerie landscape.

It was odd, Cord thought, how much the night changed things. Ordinary bushes took on menacing shapes. Landmarks moved or turned invisible. Creatures with glistening eyes moved like ghosts over a changed, almost dreamlike land. They appeared and disappeared, the coyotes and their prey, the jackrabbits. And when they paused in the hunt or the flight, they became just another dark shadow, indistinguishable from rock or plant.

He hoped that he and Earl would just be shadows when they were closing in on Horace's house, the bunkhouse, and the barn. That was Cord's wish, that they would seem only shadows against shadows. The guards, if they were looking, would not see them if their stalk was on foot and they stayed below a man's line of sight.

He went over the lay of the ranch in his mind, seeing it in both daylight and darkness.

At night, a man's vision was shortened. Even with binoculars, a man could not see well in the dark. And his line of sight would be off if he lifted a rifle to his shoulder and took aim. The dark twisted men and animals and shifted them from one plane to another. Not much, but enough that a man could easily miss any target.

Cord had the advantage, though. He knew what he was looking for. He was the hunter; Horace's men were the prey.

It was that simple.

The hunter had the advantage. Especially at night. The prey would be looking for movement and the shape of a silhouette. He would not know where to look, or exactly what he was looking for, because every blade of grass, every bush branch, was a threat.

Cord knew exactly what to look for. And he knew how to adjust his gunsights to compensate for the shift, up or down, of a man in those sights.

But he hoped that none of the guards could detect his movements. He would not be atop his horse, but a part of the land and the vegetation, a hunter on the prowl in that shadow-filled landscape that surrounded the house and the other buildings.

These were the things Cord thought about as he and Earl rode over a seemingly deserted prairie with the slight breeze in their faces and the chill searching through their clothing for warm flesh that it could cool.

When they were close enough to see the black roofs

dancing like rafts in a black sea, Cord reined up his horse and turned to Earl.

"The ranch is just ahead," he whispered to his brother. "We'll leave our horses here."

"We're going there on foot?" Earl said in an equally low whisper.

"Yes. It's the only way. We'll hug the ground, crawl if we have to. We must be very quiet, and do not shoot unless absolutely necessary. I'll show you what to do and where to be. Now, no more talk."

Earl nodded as Cord slipped out of his saddle and ground-tied Windmill to a sagebrush.

Cord knew his horse would stay there until he returned. The animal was well trained. He patted its neck and whispered into its ear as it bowed its head.

"Be a good boy, Windmill," he said. "I'll be back."

Earl tied his horse, Louie, to another bush and patted it on its rump. Then he pulled his rifle from its scabbard.

Cord left his rifle in its boot.

Earl shook his head but stayed silent.

Cord beckoned to Earl as he stood by his saddlebag on the left rump of his horse.

"I want you to tuck two of these bottles in your back pockets and follow me," he whispered into Earl's ear.

He pulled bottles from his saddlebags and handed two of them to Earl. The bottles were still wrapped in flour and coffee sacks. Earl sniffed them and nearly gagged. Then he put them into his two back pockets while Cord took two more out of his saddlebag. Cord stuffed some of the empty sacks inside his shirt as Earl watched in fascination.

Cord put two bottles in his back pockets, then walked around and took out four more, which he carried in his arms.

Using the cover of trees and bushes, Earl followed his

brother as they circled and came into the ranch compound behind one side of the barn.

There they waited, listening.

They both heard the crunch of boots. Cord motioned for Earl to stay where he was while Cord set the four bottles on the ground and edged along the back of the barn, climbed through poles that enclosed a corral, and then looked toward the bunkhouse and the main house.

He saw a man with a rifle. The man walked between the bunkhouse and Horace's house, his rifle at the ready, looking all around him. The man stopped, listened with one hand cupped to his left ear, then walked the same path again.

Cord looked to see if there were any other men, perhaps leaning against the bunkhouse or Horace's house. He waited for several minutes, but saw only the one man acting as a sentry.

He crept back around the barn to where Earl still waited.

They did not speak.

Cord crooked a finger at Earl to indicate that his brother should follow him. He picked up the bottles he had left there.

He crept to the back of the barn and squatted down. He soaked one of the rags in coal oil and stuck it under the barn. He did that to a second rag, then hunched over, walked to the corner of the barn.

There, he waited until the sentry was headed toward Horace's house. Then he hunched over and ran behind the bunkhouse, Earl right behind him.

They waited to see if the guard had heard them.

Then Cord stuffed more bottles with cloth and soaked them in coal oil.

They both hugged the side of the bunkhouse as they checked out the guard again.

When the guard walked toward the bunkhouse, Cord and

Earl dashed in behind Horace's house. They waited and listened to the crunch of boots.

The sentry stopped.

Cord's heart pounded. He heard a crinkle of paper and a rustling sound. Then the sound of a match striking sandpaper.

The guard had rolled and lit a cigarette.

There was the crunch of boots as the guard continued on his rounds.

Behind Horace's house, Cord stuffed the last of the bottles, made sure the sacks were fully drenched in coal oil. He took out his box of matches, struck one and lit the first bottle. Then he lit the others. The coal oil caught fire and streaked into the bottles. The flames licked at the wood of the house, right at the base.

He and Earl dashed back to the bunkhouse and lit the bottles that had been placed there. Finally, he set the bottles under the barn on fire. He beckoned to Earl to follow him.

They went to the front of the barn and watched the guard.

There was a crackling sound from behind the bunkhouse as the lone sentry passed in front of it. He stopped, then turned when he heard the same sound from behind the barn.

The sentry headed to where Cord and Earl waited in the shadows, hugging the wall at the front corner of the barn.

When the man was close, Cord drew his knife and grabbed the man. He clamped a hand over the man's mouth and nose.

"One yelp, and you're a dead man," Cord whispered into the man's ear.

The rifle in the guard's hands dropped to the ground. It did not make much noise.

Cord stuck the point of his knife into the man's side, just

enough so that he could feel it. He tightened his grip on the man's mouth and mashed his nose almost flat.

"You're about twenty seconds from eternity," Cord whispered into the man's ear as he ring-necked him with his right arm. He held the knife now at the man's neck, the blade pressed against his quivering throat.

"Mmmf," the man breathed as he tried to speak. As he tried to beg for his life.

"What'll it be?" Cord asked. "Life or death?"

"Mmmf," the muffled voice crept through his crushed mouth.

"You yell and it'll be the last sound you make," Cord said. Then he eased up on the grip he had on the man's mouth.

The man swallowed before he eked out his words.

His voice was scratchy and gravelly as he uttered three words.

"Go to hell," he said.

THIRTY-FOUR

Earl could not believe his ears. Cord had given the man a clear choice. Live or die.

The man was defiant until almost the very end of his life. What kind of man was this? Loyal to Horace? A fool? Mad, perhaps?

Earl saw his brother's hand mash down on the man's mouth before he could let out a yell. He saw the knife in Cord's hand poised at the man's neck. He smelled smoke and heard the sound of the flames lashing at the baseboards on the barn's back wall.

What the man did next was even more startling to Earl. It caught him unprepared.

Suddenly, the guard slammed an arm into Cord's arm. He knocked the knife away. At the same time, he drove an elbow into Cord's waist. He knocked Cord to one side and grabbed the butt of his own pistol. The sentry drew his pistol as Cord struggled to keep his footing. He shouted out a warning, calling for help.

Earl stood frozen nearby, his rifle in his hands.

The gunman started to raise his arm and bring the barrel of his pistol to bear on Cord.

Cord staggered to solid footing and slashed at the guard's arm with his knife. He drew blood as the blade slashed into the gunman's right sleeve and cut through the skin.

Cord heard the click of the hammer as the guard thumbed the pistol to full cock. In that split second, Cord knew that his life hung by a slender thread.

Earl's jaw dropped and he fumbled to bring his rifle up to a level where he could shoot his brother's attacker.

Cord swept his arm sideways in an attempt to knock the pistol from the guard's hand. His fist smacked into the guard's wrist and he gained a fraction of a second.

But the gunman whirled out of range as Earl leveled his rifle. He groped for the inside hoop of his trigger guard. His hand was shaking and he missed the aperture on the first try.

Cord sidestepped and drove in, headfirst, to smash into the gunman's stomach before he could get off a shot.

His head smashed into the guard's stomach. Cord swung his knife inward toward the man's side. The blade struck soft flesh and penetrated into the gunman's stomach.

The guard grunted at the blow. Blood spurted from the wound and he doubled over. But he still held on to his pistol.

Cord withdrew his knife blade and struck again as the guard straightened back up, his trousers soaked in blood, his wound gushing with every beat of his heart.

"Unh," the guard grunted and swung his pistol toward Cord, who was only a foot or so away.

Earl could not fix the front sight of his rifle on the gunman. He was afraid he would shoot Cord instead. The two men grappled and swung around in a circle until he could see only Cord's back. His brother was hunched over and pushing on the gunman's arm. The arm with the pistol at the end of it.

Cord knocked the arm down and away. He had gained another second or two.

But time was running out fast, like the sands in a broken hourglass.

"You, you . . ." The guard grunted and tried to step backward, away from Cord's grappling arms and the knife.

Cord did not hesitate.

He stepped inside the guard's gun arm, bumped the elbow with his left shoulder, and drove the knife straight into the man's soft belly. He plunged the knife deep. Then he twisted it and felt the man's innards open to the cutting edge of the blade. A terrible stench emerged from the man's wound as intestines emptied and gases escaped from the gunman's bowels.

The gunman staggered back. His mouth dropped open, but no sound came out past his slobbering lips.

His gun drooped, though he still gripped it.

Cord rose up above the weakened man, whose knees bent as his strength departed. He pushed the man's head back with his left hand and swung the knife in a blurred arc at his throat.

The gunman's legs gave way as the knife opened his throat. Blood spurted from the fresh wound. Cord heard a soft gurgle in the man's throat as he pitched forward on jellied knees that gave way.

The guard struck the ground with a thump and Cord stepped back. He wiped the blade on the dead man's trousers and slipped the knife back in its scabbard.

"Watch the front of the bunkhouse," he told Earl. "Shoot anyone who comes out."

Earl nodded and stepped slightly away from the barn.

The flames at the back of the barn began to crackle loudly as fire raced up the summer-dried boards and whipped toward the stored hay in the loft.

Flames rose above the bunkhouse, then crawled along the roof. The tongues of fire lapped at the dry shingles, devouring them in a rush of fire.

Cord and Earl waited, their guns at the ready. They watched as the door stayed closed and the men inside seemed oblivious to the danger.

Then they heard shouts from inside the frame building.

"Fire, fire!"

"Get out!" yelled another.

"Let me out!" a man shouted.

The front door burst open and a man still wearing his long johns dashed into the open.

More men crowded into the doorway and fought each other to burst through the open door. Behind them, flames danced at the far end of the bunkhouse and a man screamed as his clothing caught fire.

Earl raised his rifle to his shoulder and took aim at the nearest man.

Cord raised his arm and pointed his pistol at another, half-naked and barefoot.

Smoke billowed out through the open door as the flames along the roof made the shingles crackle and turn to ash.

Other men poured through the door. They coughed and spluttered as they emerged from the smoke.

And none of them were armed.

THIRTY-FIVE

Earl lined up his sights and pulled the trigger.

His rifle barked and a shower of sparks spewed from the muzzle. Hot spinning lead whirred through the dark air at his target. There was a short cry of pain and the man's legs crumpled. He went down and moaned for a second or two before he was still.

Cord picked out another man, cocked his pistol, led him as he ran, and squeezed the trigger of his Colt .45.

The man, Nestor Jones, jerked from the impact of the bullet and plowed into the ground as he hit it, a bullet hole through both lungs.

The flames on the roof of the bunkhouse surged like ocean waves across the shingles. Orange and red, they spewed smoke in their wake, thick as foam. The moonlight made the smoke glow with an eerie light, and it spread out like a fan over the running men.

Some dashed toward Horace's house, while others headed for the corrals.

Earl saw one man dart toward him, inexplicably, and he fired point-blank. The bullet struck Pete Gander on his breastbone, tunneled to a corner of his heart, and emerged under his shoulder blade. Blood squirted from both his chest and his back. He was dead before he hit the ground, and his heart stopped pumping blood within moments.

Both Earl and Cord were panting.

Cord took aim at another man, Harley Davis, who climbed up over the corral, where two horses offered some protection. Cord fired and saw Davis twitch as he clung to the top rail. Then he slowly slid down, turning toward Cord as his life slipped away.

Horace's house smoked on the back wall. Flames pierced the night with angry lashes as the fire found new wood along the sidewall.

One last man burst through the open doorway of the bunkhouse. For a moment, he was framed against smoke and flame.

Earl saw who it was and uttered a throaty cry of triumph.

It was Jessup. And he was armed. He carried a pistol in one hand, and he saw Earl at the same time Earl saw him.

Blind hatred flooded Earl as he looked at the man who had taken part in the murder of his father and the rape of his mother. The man he had chased over miles of prairie and into the hills of Oklahoma.

The flames illuminated one side of Jessup's face as he turned to see where he could run and be safe.

Earl raised his rifle again.

"Jessup, you've lived long enough," Earl yelled at him.

"You little bastard," Jessup said and stepped away from the bunkhouse. He stretched his arm out and took aim at Earl.

Earl drew a quick breath and squeezed the trigger of the Winchester. The rifle spat smoke and a vivid streak of flame as Jessup fired his pistol.

Men yelled in fear and scrambled for safety as Cord tracked them, one by one.

A shower of sparks erupted from the roof of the bunk-house and scattered against the dark sky like fireworks. The roof crackled as flames devoured the arid shingles. Flames burst through holes in the roof like golden balls of writhing fire. White smoke from the mattresses poured through those same holes and built small clouds that were pushed skyward by the rush of air issuing from within the structure.

Earl's bullet caught Jessup in his right leg as he dashed toward Horace's house. Jessup staggered as blood spurted from the wound. He stopped, whirled around, and fired another shot at Earl.

Earl jacked another cartridge into the chamber of his rifle. His teeth clamped together as he sought his target again. His eyes burned with hatred for the man in his sights.

The bullet from Jessup's pistol whirred just over Earl's head and smacked into the side of the barn.

"Damn you, Earl," Jessup shouted and thumbed back the hammer of his pistol.

Earl fired his rifle.

Jessup ducked, but the bullet smacked into his right side and he twisted in pain.

Earl moved, and Jessup's bullet plowed a furrow between his feet, dusting his boots with a thin patina of grit.

Cord dropped another man who was trying to mount one of the horses bareback. The man tumbled to the ground, his head blasted open like a ripe melon.

The rear wall of Horace's house was now crawling with fire. Tendrils of smoke streamed up over the roof and wafted into frosty cobwebs as the wind blew the fire like a squeezed bellows.

Cord wheeled to see Jessup limp toward Horace's house. Then he looked at Earl, who stood there and took careful aim.

Cord held his breath. He saw Earl's rifle belch smoke and sparks, heard the loud crack of the rifle. Jessup, he knew, didn't stand a chance. He had reached the end of his string.

Cord felt a strong sense of pride in his brother just then. It seemed as if Earl had stepped into manhood before his very eyes.

Jessup grunted as the bullet from Earl's rifle struck him just below the neck. Blood spurted from the hole like a burst fountain. He croaked a curse and his legs began to give way. The pistol slipped from his hand and fell to the flame-painted ground. He sagged to his knees, a hand going to his throat in a last feeble attempt to plug it up and stop the bleeding.

Jessup spoke no more. He crumpled forward onto his knees, then collapsed in a bloody heap.

Earl worked the lever on his rifle. He swung around, looking for another target. But there were no more men to shoot.

To Cord, Earl looked like he was disappointed. His brother had tasted blood and wanted more.

Cord was satisfied that all of Horace's men were now dead. But there was still Horace and his brother, Abner.

He looked over at the house. It was not burning as fast as the bunkhouse. But it was burning.

"Keep your eyes peeled for anyone who comes out that front door," he told Earl.

He took careful slow steps toward the house. The back wall was on fire and he saw the smoke rise up and turn to tatters in the sudden wind.

There were no lights in the house. All of the windows were dark. Strangely dark.

The front door looked oddly still, as if it the building had been abandoned like some house in a ghost town. The only sounds now were the crackle of flames as the barn began to sag and the bunkhouse raged like some fiery monster that spit out flames and spurted tongues of fire in all directions.

Cord stopped and waited. Earl came up alongside him. Both stared at the house.

"Suppose it's empty?" Earl said.

Cord shrugged. "They're in there," he said.

"Why don't they come out?"

"They sleep upstairs. Fire will get to them. The smoke. They might suffocate."

Earl stared at the house.

It was as silent as a tomb.

THIRTY-SIX

A bner, deep in the clasp of Morpheus, was the first to smell smoke.

He rubbed his nose while his eyes were still closed and he was deeply immersed in a dream. The smoke irritated his nose. He sneezed and the sneeze woke him up.

At first, he did not know that he was smelling and breathing in smoke. It was too dark to see when his eyes opened.

He reached for the matches on the little side table next to his bed. He lifted the chimney of his lamp and struck a match. He held the flame to the wick and turned it up with his free hand. The wick caught and the lamp bloomed with light. He eased the chimney back down.

He sniffed the air and knew now that he smelled smoke. He looked around the room. Behind his bed and the lamp, he saw a thin tendril of smoke that streamed through a tiny crack near the floorboard.

Abner sat up, alarmed.

In the lamp glow, he saw a fogbank of smoke rising in the room. He scrambled from under his blanket, grabbed his trousers, then his shirt, and dressed quickly. He pulled on his boots as smoke continued to seep into his room. Then he strapped on his gun belt, snatching it from the post at the head of his bed, and started for the door.

He paused at a window and cursed.

He could not see out through the boards, but he heard the ominous sound of crackling and felt the heat from the back wall. He opened his door and dashed across the hall. He tried the door to Horace's bedroom and found it locked tight.

Abner began to pound on his brother's door. He shouted as he knocked.

"Horace, Horace, let me in. Horace, fire, fire." He heard footsteps and a few seconds later the door opened.

"What in hell's the matter with you, Abner?" Horace asked. He rubbed one eye and cocked the other one at Abner.

"My room is fillin' up with smoke," Abner said. "I think the house is on fire."

Horace sniffed the air. Across the hall he could see wisps of smoke fluttering through the open door. He looked down at the end of the hall and saw more smoke oozing from the baseboards. The boarded-up window seemed to leak an orange light between the thin cracks of the boards.

Horace turned quickly and dashed back into his bedroom. Abner was right on his heels. The room was dark. Horace lit a lamp and began to pull on his trousers as he sat on the edge of his bed.

"That bastard," Horace growled.

"You think Wild set our house on fire?" Abner asked as he watched Horace pull on his boots.

"Take one of them boards off and look out," Horace said. He donned his shirt, then strapped on his pistol belt.

Abner went to a back window and pulled on the lowest board. The board was warm as he wrestled it from its nailed mooring. When he pried off the lowest board, Abner saw a bright light, then a lashing tongue of flame. He stepped back as if he had touched a hot stove.

"Good God Almighty," Abner said. "The house is on fire."

Horace turned his head and saw the glow from the burning back wall of his home. His eyes widened as he finished buckling his gun belt.

"That dirty sonofabitch," Horace said. He walked to the wall and grabbed a loaded rifle out of the gun cabinet.

"Let's go get that sonofabitch," Horace said.

They could both hear the crackle of flames and see the smoke that poured through the opening left by the slat Abner had removed.

Horace strode to the door. Abner followed him in a daze as fingers of fire groped through the place where the slat had been. The room began to fill with smoke and when they entered the hallway, there was smoke streaming from both rooms.

They raced down the stairs into more darkness. Then both entered the front room, which was also pitch-dark.

"Help me get that chair and sofa off the front door," Horace said.

"I can't see a blamed thing," Abner said.

"Light a lamp," Horace commanded as he approached the front door that was blocked with a sofa and an overstuffed chair.

Abner groped in the dark around a table where he knew there was a lamp.

He touched a box of matches, then found the base of the

lamp with nervous fingers. He struck a match, lifted the chimney, and turned up the wick. Yellow light glowed through the glass and spread out in a circle over the floor and furniture.

He heard Horace grunt as he tried to lift the chair off the sofa. He saw him bathed in a soft orangish glow from the lamplight and strode over to help him.

Abner and Horace lifted the chair, then tugged on the sofa to move it away from the door.

"He's out there, Abner. Ready to shoot us. You shoot first, you see him."

"Damned right I will," Abner said.

Horace opened the door and saw a dead man off to his right. His anger rose to a boiling point when he saw the burning barn and the inflamed bunkhouse.

Flames licked the darkness off to their right, great sashes of fire, whipped by its own wind, waving like burning flags from both structures.

Horace batted his eyes to adjust to the darkness and the flash of flames. Then he noticed all the dead men on the ground.

Abner saw them, too, and pulled his pistol from its holster.

The dead men seemed to ripple in the flaming light. They lay still, but their backs swarmed with grotesque shades of orange and blue, as if hell itself was reaching out for them.

Horace shaded his eyes to look beyond the dead men and the firelight.

He saw a pair of boots, then another.

He saw Cord and Earl just beyond the outer edge of the flaming light. Just their boots until his eyes adjusted and he saw their pant legs and then their blurred faces under hats that glowed on one side with spatters of orange that moved off and on like a railway's blinking lantern.

Abner saw them, too.

He brought his pistol up to aim and fire. It seemed to him that he was looking at two ghosts. Those two men in the shadows did not seem real. But he knew they were and he knew they meant to kill him.

As he meant to kill them.

Earl fired first. Straight at Abner. He was consumed by his hatred for the man who had led the bunch who murdered his father and raped his mother.

Blind hatred.

Except Earl's eyes could see, and as he squeezed the trigger, he felt a deep satisfaction. He also felt a power beyond himself. A power that promised justice at last for a coldhearted, greedy murderer.

Abner squeezed the trigger of his pistol just as he heard the crack of Earl's rifle. Then he felt a fist smash into his chest, a mighty fist that knocked out the breath held in his lungs.

He clutched his chest and his fingers spouted fresh warm blood, blood that pumped from the hole in his chest with every beat of his heart.

Earl saw the bullet from Abner's gun dig a chunk out of the ground between his legs. He jacked another cartridge into the chamber of his rifle.

Horace steadied his rifle on Cord, who seemed to waver in front of his eyes like some store mannequin in a window.

He also saw Cord go into a crouch and aim his pistol straight at him. Time seemed to freeze into an eternity of unreality and silence. Even the sounds of the fire diminished into a dull hum.

Sweat poured over Horace's face, dripped into his eyes. Stung like needles or biting ants.

Next to him, Abner grunted and twisted into a corkscrew under the impact of Earl's bullet.

Horace squeezed the trigger at the same time he saw

flame spew from the muzzle of Cord's pistol and he heard
the explosion of gunpowder. Cord stepped to one side, in a
crouch, his body dappled by firelight.

Horace's bullet zipped through the cloth of Cord's sleeve,
burning a path in the flesh of his left arm. Blood seeped
through the superficial wound, through the ragged tear in
Cord's shirt.

Horace felt a slap at his shoulder. It was a hard, smacking
slap that tilted his body to one side just after his rifle bucked
hard against the hollow of his shoulder. He levered another
cartridge into his rifle's firing chamber and swung the barrel
until he found Cord beyond its front sight.

He never had a chance to fire off a second round.

Cord stepped forward and stood up. He aimed at Horace's
chest and squeezed the trigger.

Abner writhed on the ground for several seconds, a rattle
in his throat, blood gushing from a hole in his back and
pumping through the hole in his chest.

Cord's bullet smashed into Horace's belly, just below his
rib cage. The lead ripped through his body and erupted from
his back, right next to his spine.

Horace uttered a loud grunt and his rifle slipped from his
hand. He doubled up in pain and clawed for his pistol, his
gaze suddenly blurred. He saw only the dancing flames from
the bunkhouse and the barn as his knees turned to gelatin,
mushy and liquid.

Cord walked up to Horace, and Horace heard the metallic
sound of the man's pistol as he cocked it once again.

Cord looked down on Horace as the wounded man sank
to his knees on the kaleidoscopic ground.

"Bastard," Horace spat through half-clenched teeth.
Teeth that were hardened in place by shoots of pain racing
through his body.

"You're plumb finished, Horace," Cord said. "A cussword ain't exactly the prayer you ought to be mounting."

"Go to hell, Wild. Go straight to hell."

Cord stepped onto Horace's gun hand, crushing his fingers until the rifle slid from his grip.

Horace did not cry out. The pain in his belly was going away, receding into the growing blackness that spread from some corner of his brain. His vision blurred as he looked up at Cord.

Cord, with a pistol in his hand, aimed straight at a point between Horace's eyes.

"Go ahead, Wild. Shoot me," Horace muttered.

"That would be too kind, Horace."

"You got me anyways."

"You made a lot of people suffer," Cord said. "Time you suffered some yourself."

"I ain't . . ."

Horace slumped down until he sat on his buttocks. One hand touched the hole in his diaphragm. Blood spewed onto his fingers. The pain returned like a searing shot of white-hot electricity, coursing through his body with crippling ferocity.

Horace uttered a groan and a sound that was more animal-like than human.

Cord pressed the snout of his pistol into Horace's forehead. Right between the eyes.

"Pull it," Horace said. "Pull the damned trigger."

"Good suggestion," Cord said.

He squeezed the trigger. His pistol roared from the explosion of power. His bullet punctured a hole in Horace's forehead and blew out a saucer-sized chunk of bone from the back of his head. Blood and brains flew into the ghastly shimmer of firelight.

Horace collapsed in a heap.

He was dead.

"You got him, Cord," Earl said as he walked over to stand next to his brother, over Horace's body.

Cord blew away the tendril of smoke rising from the barrel of his pistol. Then he hammered it back to half cock and slid it into his holster.

"I got him," Cord said, "but his evil deeds have left a big stain on a lot of lives."

"We got all of 'em," Earl said.

"We'll never get all of them," Cord said and turned away.

The death of Horace left him little satisfaction. There were more such men still walking the earth. Greedy men without consciences. Murderers, thieves, rapists.

Earl stared down at Horace, then back at the man he had killed, Abner.

"Well, we got all of these bastards," he murmured and felt a swelling of triumph in his chest. "Every damned one of 'em."

The house erupted in a fiery cloud of flame, and cartridges began to explode and shoot lead pellets in all directions. The barn collapsed in a heap of fire and ash. The bunkhouse crackled and buckled under the weight of the roaring fire.

Sparks flew into the air like a host of fireflies, dancing and dying by the dozens. They rose in the air as if they were trying to reach the sparkling stars beyond the darkness of space.

THIRTY-SEVEN

Abigail watched from the window as the dawn broke and spread a multicolored glow across the prairie. She held a cup of steaming coffee in her hand.

On the distant horizon, she saw the tiny silhouettes of two riders. Riders emerging from the dark into the dawn. That dawn with its soft glow of light that smoothed the prairie with gentle colors and streaming shadows.

Her heart quickened. She felt the beat of it in her chest and the thrum of it in her neck, just below her left ear.

She turned as she heard the *tap-tap* of booted feet on the floor behind her.

"Lelia," she said, "you're up already."

"I heard you rustling around, Ma, and I woke up. I could smell the coffee."

Abigail laughed. "Want some?" she said.

Lelia shook her head and stepped beside her mother. She, too, saw the riders approaching.

"Cord and Earl?" she queried.

Abigail nodded. "Back from the 2Bar2," she said.

"I wonder what happened there," Lelia said, a dreamy tone to her voice.

"I wonder, too." And there was her heart again, speeding up its thrum. The excitement of anticipation surged through her body like static electricity, made her flesh tingle from head to toe.

"I see you got dressed, too, Lelia," Abigail said. "Eager to see Cord?"

There was a tinge of jealousy in Abigail's voice that Lelia detected. Much to her surprise. It had not been that long since her father had been killed and her mother had hated Cord, and yet she seemed to be looking for another man.

"Not Cord anymore," Lelia said. "But his brother, Earl. I think he's sweet."

Abigail whirled around to stare at her daughter in wonderment.

"Earl? Why, he's just a boy, daughter."

"Who will grow up to be a man. An eligible man. And there are so few of them around, I can't help but be interested."

"Well, yes, I suppose you're right. Earl is a fine boy. And not much younger than you are. Of course, Jesse was older than I was when we got married, but I can see that it could be the other way around."

Lelia uttered a little laugh. "I don't see our ages entering into it, Ma. Earl is nothing like his big brother. He's polite and shy and . . ."

"I can see that you're smitten by this young man, Lelia. Just be careful, that's all I ask."

"Careful about what?"

"About how far and how fast you go with young Earl. It could just be puppy love."

Lelia snorted. "I left such things behind me long ago," she said.

"You're still too young to be thinking about all this," Abigail said.

"Maybe," Lelia said, and turned away from her mother to look out the window. "They're getting closer."

Abigail looked at the two riders, who were approaching slowly, as if out for a Sunday ride.

"That's Cord," she said. "I recognize Windmill."

The two riders lit up with splashes of sunlight. Their horses seemed to be made of burnished steel as the sun's rays rippled over their dark hides.

Abigail felt her heart quicken again. Lelia let out a sigh as she gazed at the approaching men. She clenched both fists as she silently urged them to hurry.

The horses tossed their heads as they neared the corrals with the other horses. Their tails switched as they danced their slow dance across the prairie, constrained from breaking into a run by the bits in their mouths, the firm grip on the reins by their masters.

Finally, the two men rode up to the hitch rail and dismounted.

Ernesto walked up to them, a grin on his face. He looked over at the two women standing at the window. Cord saw them, too, and waved a hand in greeting. Earl just stared, his face darkened by soot, dark shadows under his eyes.

"Morning, Ernesto," Cord said.

"You have good news, no?" Ernesto said.

"News," Cord said. "Don't know whether it's good or bad. Come on into the house with us and I'll tell you all about it."

"I cannot wait," Ernesto said as Cord and Earl wrapped their reins around the horizontal rail between two sturdy posts.

The three of them walked toward the house. Abigail disappeared from the window as she walked over to the door to open it.

"Good morning, boys," she said as she flung open her front door. "You're just in time for breakfast. I hope you're all hungry. You, too, Ernesto."

Apparently she had told Lelia to start preparing breakfast. As Cord stepped through the doorway, he saw Lelia hurrying down the hall toward the kitchen. He smelled the coffee and his stomach churned with hunger.

The three men entered the front room as Abigail closed the door behind them. They all sat down as Abigail rushed past them toward the kitchen.

"I'll fetch you all some coffee," she said. "I made a big pot this morning." Her voice trailed off.

"Boy, it feels good to sit on a soft chair," Earl said. "And that coffee sure smells good."

"You killed Horace, no?" Ernesto said with the excitement of a schoolboy at his own birthday party glowing on his leather-brown face.

"Horace is dead," Earl said. "Cord shot him right between the eyes."

"Oh, good, good," Ernesto said.

"His brother, too," Earl said.

Cord sat there in silence. He did not want to think about the killings. He smelled the lingering perfume of the two women, the wood ashes in the fireplace, the cushions and leather in the room. The acrid stench of fire and blood was still in his nostrils, in the soot that clung to his face like three-day beard stubble. His eyes were rimmed in black, like Earl's, and there was a gauntness to his face that was partly from weariness and partly from his experience at the 2Bar2, with all its horror and death.

Abigail returned with a tray bearing four cups of coffee. She passed it around to each of the men and took the last one for herself. She sat down with a huge sigh and held her cup close to her mouth and blew on it.

"I'm so glad you're here, Cord," she said. "I worried about you. Did you do what you wanted to do?"

Cord heard the banging of a pan out in the kitchen, the clang of a spoon against metal.

"You don't have to worry about Horace and his men anymore," he said to Abigail.

"He—he's dead, then?"

"He's dead."

"And all his men, too," Earl said. "And we burned down his house and his barn, the bunkhouse."

"You did?" Abigail exclaimed.

Earl nodded.

Cord reached inside his jacket and pulled out a couple of bulging envelopes. He dug into his shirt and pulled out an even fatter envelope. He set them on the table between the sofa and Abigail.

"What's that you've got there?" Abigail asked.

"One envelope has the deed to your house in it," he said. "I'll take it into town and file it with the land office in your name. No more mortgage on the JB."

Abigail smiled and draped the back of her right hand across her forehead. She looked as if she was about to faint.

"Oh, Cord, you don't know what this means to me. Thank you, thank you, thank you."

"We poured water over the strongbox," Earl said. "Drug it plumb out of the ashes of that big old house. I mean, it was still hot as hell when Cord spotted it."

Cord handed an envelope to Abigail. She opened it and drew out the papers, scanned them with widening eyes.

"Oh yes," she said. "It's here. This is it and it's still in Jesse's and my name."

Abigail laid the envelope with the deed on the small table near her.

"Which will make it easier for you to refile it for me," Abigail said.

"Exactly."

"What's in the other envelopes? That big fat one?"

Cord picked up another envelope, but left the fat one there. He handed the thinner envelope to Abigail.

"What's in here?" she asked.

"Open it," Cord said.

She opened the envelope and took out a sheaf of papers.

"Why, this is the deed to the 2Bar2," she said. "Made out to Horace Weatherall. And a bill of sale that shows he paid cash for his land."

"That ranch is yours, too, if you want it," Cord said. "There was no will, so all I have to do is file it in your name."

He turned to Ernesto.

"More ranch for you to wrastle with, Ernesto," he said. "And while I take care of those matters, you'd better get some of your hands to help you round up horses and bring them back here."

"Thirty of those horses are mine," Earl said. "And Cord's."

"They're your horses, Earl," Cord said. "You raised them, you chased after them when they were stolen."

"I will get the horses and bring them here," Ernesto said.

"I'll go with you, Ernesto," Earl said.

"I will need all the hands I can get," Ernesto said.

Abigail smiled. She continued to stare at the thick envelope, which was still lying on the small table.

Cord reached down and covered the envelope with the flat of his hand. He looked over at Abigail.

There was just a curl of a smile on Cord's lips. An enigmatic smile, Abigail thought.

Whatever was in that envelope? Abigail's curiosity bounded through her mind like a herd of gamboling antelope.

Earl cleared his throat.

Ernesto's face bore a puzzled look.

Abigail opened her mouth to speak.

There was a clatter of pewter plates down the hall.

"Breakfast's ready," Lelia called from the dining room.

Her call seemed to break the tension.

Cord picked up the envelope and stuck it inside his jacket pocket.

"I'll give you this after breakfast, Abigail," he said.

"What is it?" she asked as she rose from her chair, coffee cup in hand.

"A surprise," Cord said as he, too, arose from the sofa.

The food smell wafted down the hall as all of them headed for the dining room.

Lelia seated everyone, then sat down next to Earl.

He looked at her and smiled.

Abigail and Cord both smiled, too.

Ernesto sat next to Abigail, who was at the head of the table. Cord sat across from him on one side.

"Let us pray," Abigail said.

Everyone at the table bowed their heads.

"Ernesto," Abigail whispered.

Ernesto gave a prayer of gratitude for the food. He spoke in both English and Spanish.

Both prayers seemed fitting to Cord.

He was grateful not only to be alive, but to be sitting at table with people he cared about and who meant something to him.

"Amen," he chorused with the others.

So be it.

THIRTY-EIGHT

Cord waited until after breakfast to speak to Abigail.

"After Ernesto and Earl leave, I'll show you and Lelia what I have in this envelope," he said.

"I'm dying of curiosity, Cord."

Lelia was clearing up the breakfast dishes. Cord and Abigail sat in the front room, both sipping their last cup of coffee as beams of morning sun streamed through a pair of windows.

Cord sat on the sofa and pulled the envelope from his pocket.

"About that deed I gave you," he said. "Horace bought it from the bank, but he didn't have the JB Ranch transferred to his name. I'll see to it that you own the ranch free and clear. I'm also going to talk to the banker and tell him how much he let you down by selling your property to Horace. You and Jesse trusted him and he sold you out."

"He did. That left a bad taste in my mouth." Abigail's body shook at the thought. "That's very kind of you to do all this for Lelia and me. Stick up for us. I feel betrayed by Mr. Jeremy Conway at the bank. Jesse and I trusted him when we took out our loan. He seemed so nice."

"Turns out he was a wolf in sheep's clothing," Cord said.

Lelia skipped into the front room, a smile on her face. "Dishes all done, food put away," she said. "And I'm happy that Earl will come to work for us."

"Sit down, Lelia. Cord's going to show us what he has in that envelope."

"Oh, goody. I've been wondering what it is since you mentioned it at breakfast." She sat down in a straight-backed chair, that same happy glow on her face.

Cord knew then that she had her eye on his brother. And he could not think of a better match. Both were about the same age, and she was a nice, wholesome girl.

"There was more than just property papers in that strong-box," Cord said. "I think that you're entitled to what's in this envelope. Kind of a payback for the loss of your husband, Abigail, and your father, Lelia."

He opened the envelope and took out a stack of paper money.

"There's twenty-five thousand dollars here. Probably ill-gotten gains, but it's all yours now. This will keep you going for some time. And along with Horace's horses, you ought to do well."

Abigail gasped as Cord handed her the money. Lelia's eyes widened and her face drained of color in surprise and disbelief.

"Why, I don't know what to say," Abigail said as she took the money in both hands. "Except thank you."

"I counted it, Abigail. It's real money and it's all yours."

Abigail put the money in her lap and wiped a strand of hair from her forehead. Then she sighed, long and deep.

"Cord," she said, "I'm grateful for this money. It will help us a lot as we try to carry on without Jesse. But I can't accept all of it."

"What do you mean?" he said.

"I think some of this money should be yours. For all that you've done for us. A reward, so to speak."

Cord waved his hands at her in protest.

"No, I'm serious," she said. "I think five thousand of this should be yours, Cord. And I won't listen to a word you have to say about it."

She picked up bills and started counting them.

"Not that much," Cord said. "I'll accept some of it, but five thousand is too much."

Abigail stopped counting and looked over at Cord.

"How much, then?" she asked.

"I'll take one thousand. My fee for ridding the world of Horace and his thieving hands."

Abigail sighed again.

She counted out one thousand dollars and handed the bills to Cord.

"Thank you again," she said.

Cord took the money, folded the bills, and put them into his pants pocket.

"Oh, Ma," Lelia said, "that's so much money. Can I buy a new dress?"

Abigail laughed. Cord smiled.

"Why, darling, I'm sure we can afford a new dress for you. But I'm going to put this money in the bank. And it won't go into the one that Jeremy Conway runs. I wouldn't trust that man as far as I could throw a cast-iron stove."

Cord and Lelia both laughed.

Lelia got up and hugged her mother. Then she hugged Cord and pecked him on the cheek.

"You're my hero, Cord," she said.

Cord's face took on a rosy hue as he blushed. Then he stood up. He took the papers from Abigail, put them back in their envelopes.

"I may not see you for a while," he said. "I'm going into Cheyenne to see Conway and file your deed with the land office."

"Then what will you do?" Abigail asked.

"I'll go home and do some serious thinking," he said.

"About what?" Abigail asked.

"My life," he said. "About life itself. There's blood on my hands and I'm going to try and wash it off."

Neither Abigail nor Lelia said anything. They knew what he meant and respected him for it.

"I'll walk you to the door," Abigail said and rose from her chair. She put her arm in his and they walked to the door, where she hugged him.

"Good-bye, Abigail," he said. "If you need me for anything except . . ."

"I know," she said. "I think we'll be all right from now on."

"I'm sure you will," he said. He squeezed her hand and stepped outside.

He felt a pang of regret that he probably would not see her and Lelia again. At least not for a long time. He would arrange for a messenger to take the deeds and the filing papers back to her as proof of ownership for her ranch and Horace's. After that, he would fish and hunt, and assess his life now and for the future.

He would ride that lonesome trail of the confirmed bachelor.

He waved good-bye to the two women in the doorway and rode off toward Cheyenne.

The day was still young and he had much to do.

There was a banker to scold and papers to file.

And he had a thousand dollars in his pocket.

Enough money to last him a good long while.

THIRTY-NINE

Jeremy Conway squirmed in his chair as he listened to Cord.

"You're nothing but a scoundrel, Conway," Cord said. "You sold out a widow and an orphan to feather your own sorry nest."

"I was within the law. I sold a mortgage that was probably going into default. Nothing wrong in that."

"Legally, no. Morally, yes. The Barnes family trusted you. And you broke that trust."

"I don't have to listen to this, Mr. Wild. You have no say in my business."

"I have a say in the Barnes's holdings," Cord said. "And I just wanted you to know that the JB Ranch is on firm footing now and you will not be a part of its future growth. In fact, if I have anything to say about it, your reputation here in Cheyenne is about to take a long, hard fall."

"Are you threatening me, Mr. Wild?"

"That's a promise, Conway." Cord rose from his chair and walked to the door. He turned to face the banker before he left.

"Unlike you, Conway," he said, "I always keep my promises. Word of mouth is a powerful instrument in a town like Cheyenne."

Then he patted the butt of his pistol.

Conway blanched as Cord closed the door behind him.

And his hands began to shake.

Cord walked to the land office.

He did not see Orson Farrell, who had been watching him since Cord first entered the bank.

Farrell had been waiting for just such an opportunity ever since Wild had driven him from the 2Bar2. He had bought a used pistol in the pawnshop near the jail and thought about killing Wild if he ever showed his face in Cheyenne.

Yes, Wild had spared his life, and he should have been grateful.

Instead, Farrell knew that he had shown cowardice to a man that Horace hated. Now, he thought, he had a chance to redeem himself and claim the reward Horace had offered.

As soon as he saw Wild walk to a little building that offered courier service, he knew that it was time to show Wild that he was not a coward. He would show Wild that he was not afraid of him now that he had a fair chance.

Cord stood at the counter of Cameron's Delivery Service with a folder full of the papers he had just registered at the land office.

"Do you know where the JB Ranch is?" he asked the clerk.

"Why, yes, we have a map showing all the ranches within thirty miles of Cheyenne," the man said.

"I want these delivered by tomorrow," Cord said.

"Can do."

"I'll pay you in advance."

"That will be seven dollars and fifty cents, sir. Guaranteed delivery by four thirty tomorrow afternoon."

Cord paid the man.

"I'll need a receipt," he said.

"Certainly, sir."

The clerk wrote out a receipt and took the folder, put it in a box behind the counter. Cord folded up the receipt and put it in his pocket.

"Sir," the clerk said, "did you come here with someone else, or were you meeting someone outside after leaving here?"

"No. I came alone. Why?"

"There's a man across the street who has been watching you. I noticed him because he keeps slipping his pistol just a little ways out of his holster every few minutes."

"Is he still there?"

"Right across the street, sir. He may be wanting to rob you. We have that kind in Cheyenne, and I saw him in the Fandango Saloon last night. There were at least half a dozen known gunmen in there, but they all gave this feller a wide berth. There was something about him that smelled of trouble."

"Thanks," Cord said.

He looked out the window and saw Orson Farrell standing in front of a dry goods store, a gun belt low on his hip, his hand near the butt of his pistol. The man did not slouch but stood upright, one shoulder leaning against a post that held up a small roof affording shade for the goods on display in front of the store: linens, shoes, blankets, and bolts of cloth.

Cord stepped out of the building and looked both ways, up and down the street.

"Hey, Wild," Farrell shouted from across the street. "I'm calling you out, you sonofabitch."

Farrell's hand closed on the grip of his pistol.

"You had your chance," Cord said. "Life or death. Change your mind?"

"I ain't no coward, Wild. You buffaloed me once. Now you're goin' to pay the piper."

Farrell drew his pistol.

Passersby stopped in their tracks when they saw the pistol leave its holster.

Cord crouched and his hand streaked toward his Colt.

A woman clutched her small son in front of a nearby drugstore.

A man ducked into a haberdashery a few stores away. He carried a basket in his hand and was not armed.

Cord fired first. A split second later, Farrell shot his pistol.

People on the street ducked for cover.

Cord's bullet slammed into Farrell's chest, knocked him backward against a barrel that sprouted bolts of multicolored cloth. The bullet from Farrell's pistol whizzed just above Cord's head and whumped against the wall of a building that housed a notary public. It sent splinters flying and left a hole in one of the boards.

A woman screamed.

Cord walked across the street. He cocked his pistol.

Farrell lay sprawled on the planks that served as a boardwalk in front of Maggard's Dry Goods.

He was still alive, with blood spurting from a black hole just below his breastbone. He gasped for breath.

Cord kicked the pistol out of the gunman's hand.

"Bastard," Farrell hissed, his voice weak and breathy.

"You don't learn real good, do you, son? Looks like you're the last of Horace's men to die."

"Huh?"

"Horace is dead and so are you," Cord said.

Farrell choked on blood, and his next breath sprayed a fine mist when he tried to speak.

Cord watched him die a few seconds later.

"Go get the sheriff," someone shouted.

Cord looked at the man who'd shouted.

"And the undertaker," Cord said.

Then he walked away from the dead man and down to where his horse stood hipshot at a hitch rail. He mounted up and rode toward the street that would take him into the mountains.

He knew that there were plenty of witnesses who saw the gunfight and knew that Cord had killed in self-defense. There was little chance that the sheriff would be looking for him.

There was one less hard case in the world. And there were plenty more left in Cheyenne.

Such men gravitated to the towns like moths to a flame.

And the world was better off without them.

Cord reloaded his pistol as he rode, but he hoped he would never have to fire it again.

"Fat chance," he said aloud and patted Windmill on the neck.

Windmill whickered as he pranced toward the foothills, his rubbery nostrils already sniffing the fine clean air of the mountains.

Don't miss the best Westerns from Berkley

LYLE BRANDT
PETER BRANDVOLD
JACK BALLAS
J. LEE BUTTS
JORY SHERMAN
DUSTY RICHARDS

M10G0610

Penguin Group (USA) Online

What will you be reading tomorrow?

Patricia Cornwell, Nora Roberts, Catherine Coulter,
Ken Follett, John Sandford, Clive Cussler,
Tom Clancy, Laurell K. Hamilton, Charlaine Harris,
J. R. Ward, W.E.B. Griffin, William Gibson,
Robin Cook, Brian Jacques, Stephen King,
Dean Koontz, Eric Jerome Dickey, Terry McMillan,
Sue Monk Kidd, Amy Tan, Jayne Ann Krentz,
Daniel Silva, Kate Jacobs...

You'll find them all at
penguin.com

*Read excerpts and newsletters,
find tour schedules and reading group guides,
and enter contests.*

Subscribe to Penguin Group (USA) newsletters
and get an exclusive inside look
at exciting new titles and the authors you love
long before everyone else does.

PENGUIN GROUP (USA)
penguin.com